MW00941994

THE CHESS TEAM
(A NOVEL)

THE CHESS TEAM
(A NOVEL)

James H. Sawaski

iUniverse, Inc.
New York Lincoln Shanghai

The Chess Team (A Novel)

Copyright © 2005 by James H. Sawaski

All rights reserved. No part of this book may be used or reproduced by any means, graphic, electronic, or mechanical, including photocopying, recording, taping or by any information storage retrieval system without the written permission of the publisher except in the case of brief quotations embodied in critical articles and reviews.

iUniverse books may be ordered through booksellers or by contacting:

iUniverse
2021 Pine Lake Road, Suite 100
Lincoln, NE 68512
www.iuniverse.com
1-800-Authors (1-800-288-4677)

ISBN: 0-595-34630-8

Printed in the United States of America

This book is dedicated to Mr. O—The real Escanaba Eskymos chess coach. First my chess coach, next my colleague and chess opponent, but most importantly always my friend. You are without a doubt the greatest chess coach I have ever met.

CONTENTS

▼

PROLOGUE

▼

The intensity was more than Jim could ever handle from a chess game, yet he found himself up a rook for a pawn and victory was in his sight. For a high school player he was quite experienced at chess and knew he couldn't prematurely claim victory until his army checkmated the enemy king. As great as the odds were of winning, he couldn't let up, not now, not until the game was over.

The state team chess championship was all this team of four players from Escanaba had trained for the last three years. Now they found themselves the underdogs poised to have a chance in the last round to defeat the defending state champions from Flint. Flint donned the best player in the state for under 18 years of age, a rare chess master in Terrance Dillard. But, Escanaba countered with a sharp expert player in Junior Walters, who was the next highest rated player. The two titans faced off on first board and their game was a complicated mess of intricate ideas and deep strategies.

Jim was third in overall rank, but he loved chess probably more than Walters and Dillard combined. However, his talent and skills took much longer to nurture and what once appeared to be a serious setback had been neutralized by a tremendous inner drive to work hard and improve his game. This coupled with Walter's help, made him into a great overachiever. Without this chess mixture, Jim Berzchak was a tall skinny 'want-to-be' chess player. Today though, he had a won game, an undefeated tournament score on second board and all of his exhausting labor was going to pay off for the team.

A scrappy player named Richard Rodriguez held the third board for Escanaba. Rodriguez was a troubled young man who chased girls, drank alcohol at parties and loved to play *knockout* chess. There was no clue about his chess style. It consisted of all gambits. His affinity for risk outweighed the conservative views of his team. He either won brilliantly, or lost horribly. Unfortunately for the Eskimos, the gambit he played this round against Flint just didn't work out. His attack ran out of gas and his opponent ground him down.

Despite the loss Escanaba's fourth board Brad Bellington evened up the match. Using sharp tactics combined with a complicated opening system, he soon found himself up a queen. His game wasn't over, but everyone knew he would maintain the lead. The force of pieces he held was vastly superior and the Flint player could not find a way to make a comeback. Bellington slowly crunched his opponent move by move, taking pleasure in the fact that Flint's coach had a 'No Resignation' rule, so the only way to win was by checkmate and this he would apply in punishing fashion.

Jim looked over at his opponent and they made quick eye contact. The Flint player moved and Jim answered with an attacking maneuver and pinned his opponent's king to its back rank. The end was not too far off and he felt he could calculate every single move that could be made for the rest of the game.

"I should resign, you've got me, but my coach will kill me if I do," the Flint player whispered and smiled with an apologetic grin.

Walters examined Jim's board and then looked back at his own. Jim could feel he was thinking about the final team results and how they were in position to strike down this undefeated team.

Bellington claimed his win on fourth board and turned in his score sheet to the tournament director. With this point, their loss on third, and a 'should-be' win on second; Walters controlled the outcome of the match. All he needed to do was draw his game against Dillard and it'd be enough to outright win first place. Puzzled, Jim watched Walters get up and go to the pairing board. He soon followed. They whispered, which they weren't supposed to do, but they weren't talking about actual strategies to their games, rather they pondered *what-if* scenarios for how the final standings might play out.

"If I can draw Dillard," Walters quietly muttered so only Jim could hear, "we'll win States."

"If I win, we tie no matter what, don't we have them on tie-breaks?"

"No, that's no good, we lose on tie-breaks, see," Walters pointed to the wall chart. A quick addition of the opponent's scores showed them a tie-break meant a defeat of at least two player points in the best-case scenario.

Jim winced. "Well, I have a win no matter what, you draw him and we got it."

"Oh don't worry about that, I won't lose to Dillard, I have him psyched out. See how nervous he is? I'm the only player in this room that can stand up to him like that and he won't forget me very soon. I could even stand a chance to beat him if I worked him long enough, but a draw would be infinitely easier to achieve."

"Walters, I won't blow my game—you got my word on that."

"Okay, I'll take care of Dillard," he scratched his head and gave a strong look of excitement. "You are won, so I'll somehow force a draw with him, instead of risking it on a win. We've got this one in the bag."

A coach from another team started to approach and the two knew by experience it was time to get back to their games before the temptation of a complaint was possible.

Back at the board, Walters looked over Jim's position one more time. He reassured himself yet once more and then concentrated with full force on Dillard. Jim sat down and waited for his opponent to move. The Flint player got up to get a drink and seemed to be in no hurry to play out the lost contest.

Walters put his long fingers on his short blonde hair and sat mesmerized in deep thought. His husky football player body remained motionless like a statue for a long time, all the while Dillard rocked back and forth frantically on his chair. Jim still waiting on his opponent started to examine the Board 1 position with some depth. An anxiety attack grabbed him as he could see that if Walters sacrificed a knight for a pawn, he could at the very least set off a perpetual check and make Dillard agree to a draw. He reaffirmed his calculations and knew the state championship was really now theirs with no doubt in the equation anymore. No way would the chance be missed, if he could see the combination, so did his teammate.

Walters picked up the knight and captured his opponent's pawn with force. "Check," he announced, being extra loud while making the move. He kicked back in his chair, folded his thick arms and nodded his pug nose in a positive manner when he looked at Jim.

Dillard played a move and Walters made the next move with just as much loud force. Alarmed, Dillard pondered the position and continued to rock in his chair. After a short while, he shook his head in disgust and set his pencil down on his score sheet. "It's a draw, or we go back and forth in the same spot. Take the draw?" he offered. With no hesitation, Walters accepted the offer and left to record the result with the tournament director.

Jim's opponent finally sat back down and made a quick move without thinking. The Escanaba players were hugging each other in the corner of the room and were actually quite strident with their high-five celebration antics.

Don't blow this, Jim thought. *Bring home the bacon. Just bring home the bacon.*

His attacks proved fruitful, he snapped off another piece from the Flint player and now he was up a full rook and a queen. The end drew near, but he could barely breathe from excitement. About a dozen players from other schools surrounded the game. All took witness to a wonderful state championship run made by a small school from Michigan's Upper Peninsula that nobody knew existed, until today. Even his teammates had calmed down and watched like hawks behind him, hoping this agony would soon end and they could claim a state championship title.

'*Mate in two, I got him,*' Jim said in his mind.

He made the first move by putting his rook into proper position for a mating net. The opponent lifted his king and set it in the corner. Joyful feelings took Jim. He looked at Walters, his best friend in the whole world and with his thin shiny face gave him a stare of success. The game was all done.

With a nervous hand and awkward motion he picked his queen up, but as he moved it, the piece slipped through his fingers and fell onto the floor. The Flint player picked it up and handed it back to him. Without haste, Jim set it in place and looked his opponent in the eye.

"Checkmate!" he announced and delivered the final blow to Flint.

Jim took a deep breath to relax and smiled towards his team. Nobody moved. Something didn't seem right. The crowd remained silent and they just continued to stare at the board in awe. Jim's opponent's eyes were the size of watermelons. Nobody said anything to him and he couldn't figure out what the heck was wrong. Suddenly he felt a sharp pain to his arm, as Rodriguez swatted him.

"What?" Jim retorted. "It's checkmate, shouldn't we be celebrating?" He shot a bewildered look at Bellington who was closest to him.

However, Jim's opponent pointed at the queen, and then the situation spoke volumes of horror. In the confusion of the slipped piece, he blindly set the queen down one square farther than he meant to. Instead of winning, he actually stalemated the game. This result ended the game and tournament, leaving the two teams officially tied for first place.

"My god, I can't believe you just did that," Walters exclaimed, not believing what had happened. "You choked and gave them our state championship on tie-breaks!"

The trophy ceremony followed minutes later and the Eskimos dragged forward in a dismal mood. Walter's words wouldn't stop ringing in Jim's ears and continued to stun him. He didn't cry, but he wanted to. This was not how it was supposed to be. To make matters worse, they all had to stick around so he could be presented with the best second board trophy. Despite the goof up draw, he was far ahead of any other second board in competition and he clearly shined as a valuable player only to meet such fine success with the most disastrous of finishes.

Some players from other teams started to snicker when the presentation was made, but Walter's flexed his muscular arms and pointed for them to stop or they'd pay. They quickly complied.

Jim gave the presenter a fake smile, and barely shook hands when they awarded him the sparkling and glossy trophy. When the ceremony ended, the team left out the side doors and nobody talked to Jim on the way to the hotel. Walters gave him a pat on the back that meant he'd still be friends, but tomorrow not today, the loss just felt too painful.

While the team packed their luggage into the van at the hotel, Jim noticed a dirty garbage dumpster nearby in the parking lot. He studied his trophy and read the gold plated inscription, BEST 2nd BOARD—MICHIGAN HIGH SCHOOL STATE TEAM CHESS CHAMPIONSHIP—1989. With a deep breath and a heavy mind, he walked over to the dumpster, lifted the lid and pitched the trophy.

Once in the van, he threw his duffle bag of clothes in the back area, set up a tape in his cassette player and waited for the other players to finish packing. He occupied the farthest seat back and nobody sat near him. Sliding his sunglasses, he put his headphones on and blasted his ears with music. Tears rolled down his cheeks and pain filled his stomach, but nobody talked to him. Nobody talked to him the whole trip home.

Chapter 1

▼

The Captain Comes Home

The phone rang, but Jim Berzchak was far more interested in the chess position he suspended on a mental board inside his mind. He had been able to add startling detail to this visual image with letters a through h running alongside White's edge of the chess board and the numbers 1 through 8 the opposite direction. Amazing enough he could rotate this position back and forth and wondered how the heck after so many years of rigorous mental training he managed to do this.

The game he studied came from a favorite book of his, about Wilhelm Steinitz who many considered the first world chess champion in the late 1800s. Although his mental acuity was strong enough to see the whole game in his mind, he felt he needed more work yet in retention of games. He recalled 15 years ago in high school Walters could visualize a board exactly like this. However, what set Walters apart from most regular players was his phenomenal memory, borderline photographic, a gift. This frustrated Jim, but he vowed to never give up until he could at least remember enough to get him into the realm of elite chess players.

The beeping noise of his answering machine finally threw his concentration off and the pieces in his brain seemed to fall over in a blur.

"Hello?" he picked up the phone and interrupted the machine. He shut it off and gathered his wits.

"Hi, is this Mr. Berzchak?" a soft teenage voice asked.

"Yes," he replied fast and distracted. This was the only word he seemed to be able to get out as fretful nerves kept him on edge.

"Mr. Berzchak, my name is Greg LeBlanc, my dad works with you at the college cafeteria. He says you know how to play chess really good."

Jim tried to think of whom Greg's dad might be and it didn't take long to realize it was the guy they called Ole Cookie because of his senior food service days in the Marine Corps back during the 1980s Granada military campaign. The nickname certainly was unusual, but nobody gave him any flak about it. His meals were so well prepared and delicious, no soldier would dare risk offending Ole Cookie, not if he wanted to keep eating well. However, he was 6 foot 8 and built like a big wrestler and this no doubt also helped keep unwanted comments away.

"Ole Cookie is your dad?" Jim asked a little more comfortable now, the feeling of unknown not so bad.

"Yes he is, and he says you play chess every day," the young man answered, trying to gain conversation.

"Yeah, yeah," Jim patted his untamed brown hair. "You're dad talks about you a lot, says you're really good at math and you like aeronautics," he paused, took a short breath as a new wave of nervousness captured him. "What do you want?"

"Ah, Mr. Berzchak would you start a chess team at the high school? I love to play, and there are others that do too, but we don't know what to do to get organized."

Jim's breathing about ceased. The question was so unexpected he couldn't reply. Instead he stood by the phone stupefied by the strange request.

"Hello?" Greg continued.

"Uh, I," he couldn't get the words out. The stress seemed unbearable.

"Please, my dad says you're really good, he watches you play all the time. He says you are a purist, that you love the game. Please coach us?" Greg begged.

Jim wondered what the heck he meant by being a purist. Playing all the time wasn't totally true either, he only read chess books continuously on his lunch and breaks, but never played in public, only against the computer alone at home. Nobody around could even hold a candle to his chess strength any way, but even if they could, chess to him was too personal to share with most others.

"Well, I just don't think it's feasible," he tried to let the kid down easy. "Greg, I just don't really play seriously anymore. I, well uh, I just don't. It's too hard to explain, I'm sorry."

"Is it true you really don't need a board or pieces to play?"

Caught off guard, Jim wasn't sure how to answer. "Sort of Greg, I haven't played tournament chess in a very long time, 15 years." These words seemed easier to get out. "It's a long story, you don't want to hear it, but the bottom line is I just don't play anymore. Starting a chess team, I'm sorry it's out of the question." He could tell he hurt the young man's feelings.

"Well, if you change your mind, will you tell my dad at work?"

"Sure, I'll talk to you later Greg, good-bye," he finished and hung the phone up in its place.

He couldn't help but feel he did something wrong. Sure, the natural thing to do is say no when someone asks for something spur of the moment like that. Realistically though the kid had no clue of what kind of commitment he had just asked for. Yet, deep down he admired Greg's ambition for giving him a call and showing enterprise.

Jim's old coach retired from his teaching position a few years back and moved to Florida. The old high school chess club and team folded a short time later. The huge 30-year surplus chess club budget dissolved quickly into the athletic fund. With no money or support, nobody in the Escanaba area had the knowledge of pulling the task off, except for Jim.

One thing he didn't like was that chess didn't get the respect like the big spectator sports of football, basketball and hockey. Instead chess players were mainly noted as 'geeks' or 'nerds' and even though he knew he fit that stereotype, most other chess players didn't. His old teammates showed this first hand.

Walters led the group in prestige as he sat on the verge of becoming a captain in the United States Navy. Rodriguez ended up managing a casino in Las Vegas and made more in bonuses than Jim made the last five years in food service. Bellington became a pharmacist and owned his own little drug store in a small town. All of them claimed above average success, all had great incomes and none of them lived any image of the word 'geek'.

Most of the time it seemed that when chess had some success, people would nod, even give a congratulating handshake, but nothing more. The impression lasted minutes if not seconds and then it would always be off to other things. Never did the big game World Champion Gary Kasparov won to clinch first place at Linares ever become big talk. If Brett Favre threw for 300 yards in football on any given Sunday he was a deserving hero, but a grandmaster chess player didn't get accolades for spectacular performances. He was afraid that chess might never get that kind of honor in the United States. Deep down he didn't stop hoping it would. After all, there was enough room for chess in people's busy lives. He still remained an ardent Green Bay Packer football fan, however only after four or five hours of studying chess on a Sunday morning.

He couldn't ever recall meeting a person that did not like chess, yet he never met many people that loved it either. 'Monopoly' the board game seemed to come to most people's minds when he'd talk about chess. Little did they know that if they truly understood the action, upon viewing a grandmaster game the contest could equally match the excitement of an entertaining football game.

The discomfort of bad communication about chess actually forced him to stop talking about the game to most others. They just didn't understand and even if they were experienced players, they didn't seem to understand how the game truly worked. He didn't despise this. Rather he pitied it. Something so beautiful like a mate in three combination could easily possess the striking beauty of any mathematical theorem, painted picture, piano recital, or 3rd down blitz. Chess had this canny ability to be art, but also contained the dual role of sport and this is what made Jim love the game so much, because it did what most other activities couldn't.

Glancing at his computer, he noticed an email from his good friend Walters. He knew the seaman's leave time neared and he was coming home this year for a visit. A quick double click and the message appeared on the screen.

MADE RANK OF CAPTIAN!!! GET VACATION BEFORE TAKING COMMAND. CAUGHT A NAVY FLIGHT FROM BAHRAIN. LEAVING WITHIN THE HOUR. SHOULD BE HOME AT 8 PM EST DUE TO TIME DIFFERENCE. MY MOM IS AWAY WITH MY SISTER IN WISCONSIN, SHE'S HAVING HER THIRD CHILD (YIKES!) WILL HAVE TO HANG OUT WITH YOU THE WHOLE TIME. MAYBE HIT A CHESS TOURNAMENT. DYING TO PLAY. SEE YOU SOON—WALTERS

"Eight tonight?" Jim gasped to himself. "Why that's like in a few hours!"

Panic grabbed him, but he calmed. Walters was a blanket of security for him, a great friend. Jim had no siblings, but Walters basically was his big brother in most senses. Back and forth he cleaned up his apartment and took a trip down to a small party store to get different household supplies.

After having the place dressed up the best he could, he kept wondering that he had missed something. Then he noticed the table stood vacant with its two lonely chairs. The chess set, he remembered. He hadn't used one in so long he hoped his old 'Staunton' regulation set still held up in decent shape. Pulling the dusty thing out, he laid the black and white pieces on the table in ordered fashion. To his relief it only needed a speedy shine that he administered. Each refreshed piece gleamed like he had bought it brand new. He next set each one on the playing board, exactly in the center of each square, and adjusted the playing surface a number of times to make sure that it had perfect symmetry with the table on all sides.

The board, table and chairs looked in near perfect position. That left only the chess clock to take care of. He pulled the old mechanical clock out and looked at the grimy thing. It had two faces, one on each side for each player. With a rag and cleaner it didn't take long to make them shine. He worked the two buttons at the top that each player would push after a move. After he wound up each side the device began to work properly but felt rough to the touch. A little household oil smoothed things and 'Ticker' looked to be revived to its old glory days. Right next to the dark pieces, on the right hand side he placed the clock exactly in the center of the board and the scene could not be more ideal for Walter's visit.

Time off at the cafeteria had to be approved so he called his boss and asked for a vacation week off. Jim apologized for the unplanned notice, but explained that his friend had unexpectedly come home from military duty and the occasion warranted the request. His boss readily accepted because Jim worked hard and had only ever asked for time off once before. For a line cook he had more vacation time in the leave bank than almost all the other employees at the cafeteria combined.

All the chores had been completed and 8:00 PM still lingered a couple hours a way. He decided a quick nap would be the best way to use the extra time and he lumbered in deep rest on his sofa.

Pound, Pound, Pound, he awoke to hear someone rapping on his door. He looked at the clock quick, '8:26 PM' it read. Realizing he slept much longer than intended, he jumped to his feet quick and checked the security peephole in his door. Outside he could see a clean-shaven burly man in a dark blue uniform with a military duffel bag at his side. Many medals and ribbons shined brightly on his uniform and he looked almost like a giant sports trophy. However, only Junior Walters could wear that much military hardware and not look gaudy. Anybody that knew the man also knew that spectacular was the only way to describe his work dedication. Senior officers would call him '24-7' because he'd literally work 24 hours a day for the whole week if that's what it took to get the job done right.

Jim opened the door and the two friends made eye contact. Much time had passed since they'd seen each other. He offered his hand in greeting and almost thought he had stuck it a in a vice grip.

"It's so good to see you Berzchak," Walters exclaimed. "How you been?"

Nerves took Jim, and he almost couldn't reply with words. He felt so happy to see his friend.

"Still timid aren't you? Dang, you're as thin as when we were in high school. Come on, let's go get a steak dinner."

"Uh, I've got some here," Jim calmed. "Steaks I have that is. I get them at the cafeteria at cost, quite good. Let me cook them up. It won't take long. I have a great potato dish that will go great with it, you'll love it." He didn't even think twice and went to the kitchen.

"Wow, you cook at home now? I would have never expected that. Let me know if I can help with anything then?"

"No, don't worry about it. I do this stuff for a living. Not to be politically incorrect, but women's work, who would have thought hey?"

Walters saw the chess set and it slowed him down. Memories of fond trips he and Jim took long ago started to flash back to him. The two were inseparable at that time and had a chess link that made them into best friends. He continued to look at the board while Jim cooked and knew that chess had been lost and missing in his busy work life.

"Wanna go to a chess tournament this weekend, I was looking in my 'Chess Life' bulletin and it says the Michigan Open is this weekend?" Walters asked. "When's the last time you been to a tournament anyway, what's your rating?"

"Heh," Jim replied, as he made some final preparations. He concentrated on the food as it cooked fast and the feast would soon be complete. "1856 is my rating, just like it was after my last tournament," he said and stopped. Nerves and fear grabbed him, "1989 State Championships."

"What? I thought you told me in letters and email that you were playing again."

"Internet and computer chess. Yeah I'm sharp, I can get well over master level in blitz chess, but we both know that's not real chess," he continued and added the final touches to the meal. "Besides, uh, you know how I am, just too quirky."

"Bah," Walters disagreed, but was cut off as Jim placed a medium-well steak cooked to perfection with extra fixings in front of him. "Oh my that does look good."

"Steak sauce?" Jim offered.

"Never. Butter, salt and pepper only please."

"You said awhile back the doctor wanted you to watch your cholesterol didn't you?"

"Yeah, but you only live once right?" Walters replied.

Walters took his knife and spread a huge slab of butter on his steak. Every bite melted in his mouth. The meal tasted delicious, but he couldn't resist making the first move on the chessboard since the white pieces stood on his side.

Without hesitation Jim replied with a move Walters totally did not expect, but a move he clearly knew how to deal with. A couple more moves followed and Walters looked stunned.

"Since when do you allow a Ruy Lopez?" he asked about the choice of opening moves. "You were a Caro-Kann guy years ago."

"I still play the Caro, just wanted to see your old Ruy line."

"Tisk, tisk, you know the Exchange Variation like this gives White an edge and easily planned game. How do you expect to win?"

Walters continued with his next move, so far the game outside of its surprising direction, was quite routine and his memory aided him without serious effort. Move after move the two played on, quick and easy, almost as if they had planned to recite memorized poetry. Finally, Jim broke the script by playing his knight to the f4 square on the 17th move.

"What the heck is that?" Walters exclaimed in surprise. "Hmmm, everyone knows you need to get ready and castle queenside." As he examined the position, dilemma after dilemma silently filled his mind. "Maybe that isn't such a bad move." He took the knight with his pawn.

Jim stayed calm. He knew taking the knight enabled him to attack ferociously on the kingside. However, with Walters as an opponent, one never knew what ingenious defense he could come up with in a spontaneous manner. Continuing, he brought his Queen in for the kill. Walters moved and then Jim moved his bishop that added more painful aggression towards the opened up king.

"Wow, I must really be rusty. How the heck did you learn to play like this," he noted and moved. "Oh man, it's mate in four isn't it."

"Yep," Jim replied. His mind was stunned at the success. "I can't believe I just beat you."

"Bah, it was luck. I'm rusty you know. I haven't played seriously in many years. Heck, I work 12 hours every single day, sometimes a lot more you know that."

"Yeah, I suppose," Jim nodded in a modest headshake, but could feel Walter's moves were still solid enough to be considered good. "You're just rusty."

"Set them up again," Walters demanded and switched the board around. The loss had bruised the captain's ego.

Jim made the first move, and put Walter's on defense because the move did not correspond with his old opening repertoire from high school.

"What's this, you never play 1.e4 like that. When did you start playing this?" Walters asked. "This isn't your style you know—you're a passive player not aggressive."

"I know," Jim took a drink of water. His nerves were starting to affect him. He didn't want to make his friend angry. "I just got tired of having to play 55 moves a game to win or draw. 1.e4 makes most of the games a lot faster and it's much easier to understand."

"Sure, after all these years, now you finally listen to me," he replied and smiled. "All right, but you know my Sicilian is dangerous."

The truth couldn't be more evident. Walters only lost one game in his whole high school career with the Sicilian Defense, he even drew Dillard with it, but Jim had a good plan up his sleeve. An old Mikhail Tal game with the Chekhover Variation seemed to come to his mind. Tal had been a great world champion in his day and Jim knew the theme of the opening quite well, and knew it was extremely difficult to beat. Maybe Walters would show him a creative defense.

The two held such familiarity with the opening that they ripped off the first 10 moves in seconds. A few more moves went by and Walters started to slow down and think. He played a pawn to h6 to harass a bishop and Jim just stupefied him by replying with the h4 pawn and ignoring the threat.

"Come on, that gives me a bishop for free. You can't play that," Walters laughed. "For a minute I thought you were playing good."

Jim couldn't understand how Walters didn't see the attack he had sprung. Taking the bishop was exactly what the grandmaster did versus Tal and it led to resignation six moves later.

"I don't understand?" Jim puzzled. "That loses Walters, doesn't it?"

"What are you talking about? I can hold that piece any day of the week," he burst his chest in confidence. "All I have to do is grind things down and I'm up a piece, a won endgame. I'll have to show you I guess."

Jim didn't know what to make of his good friend's statements. Sure, the position held extreme tactical secrets, but this position had been proven already and further, he knew the secret to proving it. He didn't have the strength to argue, but rather brought his rook timidly over to attack his buddy's king. Three more moves followed and Walter's face turned red. With his king hopelessly surrounded by enemy forces, he tipped it over.

"More," Walters demanded setting up the pieces.

The two battled on all night long. They didn't talk about old times, they didn't catch up on new lives, and they didn't even talk to each other. Rather they enjoyed their first love, the game of chess the whole night and Jim beat Walters every single game.

"I can't be that rusty," Walters admitted. "Berzchak, you're better at chess than I am. I still know those lines well enough and dang, I can't believe you cleaned me up like that."

"No, it was just luck. I'm having a good night. You'll get me back tomorrow."

"Trust me you are at least playing senior master level chess. You've made it and as much as I hate to admit it, you did it without me."

"We both know I wouldn't be anything without you Walters, you taught me to play."

"Yeah, I taught you to play, but dang, you took it to a whole different level." Walters couldn't seem to get over his astonishment. "Berzchak, we gotta get you to a tournament." He opened his chess magazine. "Kalamazoo—Michigan Open."

"No, no, I'll go, but I just want to watch you play."

Walters shook his head. "We gotta get some rest, dang we stayed up all night."

"Sure, but I'm not playing in that tournament."

Walters grabbed his bag and his toothbrush. "Oh yes you are, I insist."

"I really don't want to play."

"Listen," Walters stopped to understand the reluctance and personality troubles displayed by Jim. He decided to play a firm hand Jim could not deny. "Me and you are a team and one of us is going to win that tournament. You're going and you're going to play." He again demanded and disappeared into the bathroom.

Jim's nerves swelled. The thought of going to a rated tournament scared his wits. The Michigan Open fielded at least 100 players. His breathing became tight and he thought he might even pass out. Somehow, he needed to talk his friend out of this crazy idea of playing in a chess tournament.

CHAPTER 2

▼

A RETURN TO
TOURNAMENT CHESS

"Wow, look at that Mustang," Walters admired at Jim's car. "What is it an 87'? I always wanted one of these since high school."

The car held a beautiful shade of candy apple red and when the two got inside it started like a charm. The power of the engine roared them down the road, and they set off for Kalamazoo.

"This thing is like brand new," Walter's stated. "How many miles you got on this thing?"

Jim looked at his dashboard, "sixteen thousand three hundred and two," and then continued his careful driver stance with his hands at ten and two on the steering wheel.

"And how long you had this thing?"

"Just about twelve years."

Sadness overtook Walters a little bit. He took a crisp look at his friend and felt some regret. He saw a supreme kind person that had been living his life in a mere shell, tucked away from the rest of society.

"Hey Berzchak," he said, "you ever pick up any women in this thing? My goodness, it's literally a chick magnet."

Jim laughed two short breaths and hung his head low in response and Walters deduced the answer.

"You ever date or see any girls?"

Again, with head low, Jim kind of tried to avoid the topic. Walters could see him shake and decided not to press it.

"Well, one of these days, some good looking gal is going to be beating your door down. With a car like this and how good of shape it's in, yeah, it'll happen."

"I doubt it," he modestly replied. "It's just like the days of old, no luck. I don't even ask anymore, it's always 'no' for an answer. I won't give up though, how about you?"

"Me?" Walters squinted with surprise. "Yeah, I get women in every port we stop at, tons of them. Especially the foreign girls, they go nuts for us. Nothing ever serious—but even that's possible."

"Must be nice to have all the girls you want. All I'd love to have is one loving wife. That's it."

"She'll come buddy, trust me, she'll come. I'm a true believer that there's a person out there for everyone. What about money? How you doing there?"

"I'm doing pretty good. I'm making $8.50/hour as a line cook, which is the max pay, because I've been there 14 years. Hard to believe I got that job while getting my associate's degree at Bay hey?"

Walters cringed. He was making a good $40/hour more than Jim and just didn't have the heart to tell this fine and caring person the difference. Staying in one place haunted Walter's thoughts. He had literally seen the whole world in the last 15 years touring to Bahrain, India, France, Italy and the Philippines. No way could he comprehend being stuck in Escanaba his whole life, and he didn't feel it could be healthy for a young man to just waste away like Jim had been doing.

"How about your bills?" Walters asked.

"Oh, I'm doing good there, only room and board. I've got a lot saved up in my savings account, about $4,000."

Again Walters had all he could do to not get discouraged. He had almost a quarter of a million dollars in his IRAs through the military from bonuses and aggressive investing. However, he did feel good Jim made an initiative to not be wasteful and to save for the future. He knew the reality of lifestyle pretty much existed in one's perception. A person didn't realize they were poor if they actually thought they were doing well with their money and how bad could that be? Jim did own one heck of a beautiful car.

"How about your health?" Walters asked. He thought he'd probe in one more area he had some concern.

"Health?"

"Well, you know, your well being, everything's okay right?"

"Interesting you should ask. I just had my yearly exam from the college. Before the fall semester every year they offer a physical and mental health clinic for employees to take advantage of. The physical went great, a little low on body weight, but fit. Mental wasn't horrible, the psychologist said I suffer a bit from nerves, but it's not like I'm neurotic or anything. He said I do have slight depression, but from his tests I don't require medication. Lots of fishing and fresh air he recommended," Jim finished.

Walters felt glad he had asked and felt even better that Jim's health was in reasonable condition. The two continued to catch up on old times and Jim even loosened up and became his old self again to a large degree. They drove for hours on end, stopped at several gas stations and restaurants and then followed their directions to the playing site hotel. Upon arriving and checking into their double room, they set up a board and started to practice for the tournament. For at least a day, the two seemed to be back in the reality of their early adulthood years when they competed on the chess circuit.

Morning soon followed and the two found themselves at an I.H.O.P. eating the inexpensive scrambled eggs, bacon and pancake special. The affordable price held no reason to why they ate this on this trip. Rather they ate it in remembrance of the good old times when they hopped in the vehicle and drove to chess tournaments. Usually these trips lacked the proper financing and they would barely have enough cash to pay for gas, entry fee and a little food.

On many trips they slept in the car even in the winter to save room costs, and other times they'd hardly scrape up enough change to share a small meal. The early days of their chess youth were rough and tough, but completely satisfying in terms of memories. Once in awhile, good fortune would bestow them in prize money. One time Walters won a big $350 first place prize, while Jim took third for $100. The chess kings felt so rich; they got a hotel room and stayed an extra night. They proceeded to be like real kings and headed to a fancy steakhouse. After eating until it hurt, and hurt bad, they lounged at the hotel like lazy lizards in front of the television, relaxing and watching movie after movie all the while basking in their mental greatness.

After breakfast, the two returned to the hotel and the smell of competition entered their noses. A tournament chess player could spot other chess players a mile away, and Jim's senses peaked. He didn't even know who any of these people were, yet he could almost tell their playing strength on looks alone. Goose bumps grabbed both of them. They could not believe they had actually entered a tournament again after such a long departure.

"Name, USCF-number and expiration on the card please. Rating if you know it here, and of course, the $35 entry fee." The tournament director announced when they walked up to the registration table.

The two printed their names on the cards, put their ID numbers appropriately and each checked the 'Life Member' box on the card. With $35 cash each, they completed the process and were entered to play.

"Couple of life members. Good, won't have to process anything. Saves me time and trouble," the tournament director continued. "Extra rules are on the post-it board. Pairings will be up in 20 minutes, everything you guys need will be on that wall there," he pointed and then turned his full attention to the next player in line.

The two went to the hotel restaurant for a couple cups of tea and after a brief relaxation came back to the tournament room. There were about 60 chess sets and pieces all set up, with display cards in numerical order all under a room that had splendid lighting from above. An average person could read for 15 hours straight under such good conditions and Walters gave Jim a smile, they both knew this would suit them well.

Jim grabbed 'Ticker' out of his backpack, and they both headed to the pairing charts to see what boards they would play on as well as their opponent's names and ratings.

"Will you look at that," Walters stuck his finger on the top name, "Dillard. Oh he's been working at his game, look at that, almost a couple hundred points higher than when I played him last."

"His strength shows, but look we're right below him at 2nd and 3rd rank," Jim noticed. "Dillard Jr. is 4th, isn't that interesting."

"That's just crazy, what is that kid maybe a young teenager tops? And he's almost as high rated as us? No doubt the old man trained the kid well, but they're in for a rude surprise. Berzchak, if I don't win this tourney, you will."

"Well, Dillard is one, you're two, I'm three and that kid is fourth. Dang, out of almost 100 people here, who would have figured that?" he looked at more names to see if any of the old Escanaba teammates had made it. At the very bottom his eyes caught a surprising name. "Look at this, Greg LeBlanc—Escanaba MI."

"What?" Walters reflected. "Do you know him?"

"Well, I work with his dad at the college. He called me up and asked me to start a chess team at Esky High. That is just too crazy eh?"

"What'd you tell him? No?"

"Yeah, I told him no," Jim retorted with surprise. "Come on Walters, you know the disaster I live with everyday."

Revelation showed on Walter's face. He wondered if it could be true that Jim still suffered from that horrible loss of States at the hands of Flint. This matter held serious consequences and he wanted to confront his friend about it soon, however the tournament director started to make his opening announcement and the players crowded the room and found their respective spot at their boards.

Jim sat down at Board 3, while Walters sat across the table to his left. Over to his right was where Dillard Jr. would be sitting, and Dillard Senior had a single table waiting for him just a few feet away. The first board of a tournament usually sat alone as a privilege to the player that had the highest rating or the best score of the tournament.

"Hey Jim," Ole Cookie bellowed and raised his hand for greeting.

"Hi," he replied quietly, stress taking him firmly as he shook hands. He just remained quiet not knowing what to say and he certainly didn't have the knowledge of manners to introduce Walters in greeting.

"We didn't know you'd be here," Ole Cookie continued as Greg approached with him. "This is our first tournament. Do you think my son here will do all right?"

Greg kind of waved and Jim replied with a half wave of his own and gave a psychic stare of bewilderment. Greg sat down next to Jim on Board 4 and started to get his pen and score-sheet out for the game. Ole Cookie gave his son a pat on the back with is long arms, and then feeling out of place took off his 'Army' baseball cap, rubbed his short black hair and then sat down over on the other side of the room.

The top ranked players usually got paired with beginners in the first round, to sort of give them an easy victory for a fast start. A strong player though never relaxed, upsets did abound, but it did appear that Greg had been selected as one of the sacrificial lambs by the unkind formula of the Swiss pairing system.

Dillard and his son strutted into the room like they owned it and disappointment showed on their faces. They were tall and thin, dad now balding, glasses, but an air of confidence beamed from him. Son looked nearly an exact replica of dad, yet with more vitality and a full head of hair. They both wore plain clothes and their appearance proved simple. One could easily tell chess meant everything to them. Although the son seemed similar to his father, he wore a much more arrogant grin on his face.

"Well, well, well, if it isn't the long lost crew from Escanaba," Dillard Senior stated in a dull tone without offering a handshake. "Terry here," he pointed to his son, "is quite disappointed to not be at the second board here closer to me."

"That's just a darn shame now isn't it," Walters chimed back. "I guess he'll just have to earn that privilege."

"It's okay dad, I'll beat all these guys and it'll be me and you in the finals," Terry remarked, as he sat down across from Greg.

Walters laughed, but Jim just froze. Greg had no clue what was going on and Jim saw confusion in the kid's eyes. He shook his head in a meaningful way to let him know not to worry about the comments and to just try to play the toughest he could against Terry.

"Now son, you just take it easy on these fellows," Dillard Senior requested in a calm manner. "They were pretty good years ago, but they're not serious about it like we are. They don't win like avid players do, they're here to have fun and it's always fun to teach them a few lessons."

Walter's face turned a deep red and even Jim's inner response held anger inside towards the off the wall comments. Players started to file in and it didn't take long for all the chairs in the large banquet room to be filled. Table after table the players waited patiently for the tournament director to give the sign to begin, yet at the top boards animosity still ran in everyone. Somebody would prove to be the best and ultimately back up their chess strength with not just words or feelings, but with results.

"Shake hands, you may start the clocks," the tournament director announced.

The cadence of many chess clocks pulsed in the air and then pure silence befell the entire room. The tournament had started.

CHAPTER 3

▼

TOUGH PLAY

The players moved fast at the higher ranked tables, except for Greg's game. Jim noticed the youngster double checked everything on the board and then did the same with his score sheet. He always favored this extra careful method in his own games and it proved to be an agreeable point about the kid.

Walters enforced checkmate on his low rated opponent, much quicker than anyone else at the top. Dillard Senior didn't wish to be outdone too badly and followed by gaining a rook advantage. Jim knew by move nine that he had a strategically won position, however, it would take a good 40 moves of flat execution and solid prophylactic playing to force an actual checkmate.

The only game left of any interest was on Board 4. Terry had started off with the Fried Liver Attack and sacrificed a knight for two pawns to try and go for a knockout blow on Greg's king. At all times there only seemed to be one move that would save the game and each time Greg inexplicably found it to keep his position alive.

An hour of solid playing passed and Dillard Senior finally polished off his opponent. His game had been won for quite some time, but the guy just wouldn't resign. Jim found himself with a similar dilemma, he held two extra pawns, and virtually had a death lock on his opponent, but the player had the right to hold out until checkmate. Greg's game had turned into one of trench warfare. He still held a tiny advantage deep into the middle-game and Terry's face started to show the signs of frustration, as normally the game should have been in his hands by this time.

Finally after a deficit of a fifth pawn from the board, Jim's opponent decided the game by tipping his king over in resignation. He filled out the scorecard properly and turned it in to the tournament director. Instead of meeting Walters at the room to rest, he went back to the tournament hall to watch Greg play his game. Terry seemed to be in a mode of desperation and started a queenside pawn-storm to bring the game into another dimension. Again, Greg arose to the challenge and staved off the attack. The game battled back and forth as both players refused to give up or make a mistake. Even Dillard Senior walked by and felt dismay that his son hadn't defeated this simple beginner by now.

With Terry slowly running out of ammunition, his position started to deteriorate and he knew a couple more moves and he'd be beaten. He battled on and Jim noticed him tap his foot on the ground in a rhythmic manner. Terry started to make his moves much faster and then Jim noticed Greg's clock was down to the one minute left. The strategy now became apparent; he would try to blitz Greg out of time and win the game that way.

A little red flag right above the top of the clock hung in the balance on the long hand and there couldn't be more than half a minute now. Jim knew Greg didn't see it and even by now, with five more moves to make in time control, he'd surely blow the lead. Inadvertently he gripped 'Ticker' tight in his own hands, turned it back and forth, then stopped because maybe Greg would see him do this and it would unfairly remind him that he was low on time and Terry could raise a complaint.

Each second ticked by and the stress nearly made Jim collapse, while the same could almost be said for Terry as his nervous foot pounded on the floor more pronounced. Greg seemed calm and made a solid attacking move. Not even a second went by and 'snap' Terry made his move in an instant. Only now did Greg realize something was up and raised his eyebrows and scratched his blonde scalp in surprise to see his time problem. With one single glance at the board he fired a move. Like lightning Terry answered and Greg matched his speed. Terry then stopped, thought for a minute and got up and went to get a cup of water.

'*That tricky little bugger,*' Jim thought. He recognized what deception Terry had in mind and had used the same ploy many times himself. Whenever an opponent sat on the verge of their time expiring and they knew it, one of the best psychological strategies was to let them think about it for a while. This stunt could be compared to calling a time-out and icing an opposing kicker in football before they had a chance to boot the game winning field goal.

Terry strolled back to the table, took a sip of his water and started to think. Jim saw a trap he could use and it seemed to occur to Terry too as he made the foreseen move. Greg could see something wrong with the position and realized it flat out required time to solve. The newcomer didn't have the background like these top players and he glanced at Jim and shook his head in apology.

The little red flag fell and wobbled several times until Terry stopped the clock for good. Greg offered his hand, but Terry just handed him the scorecard for his signature to prove his victory. After signing it, Greg offered his hand again and Terry refused with a grumpy glance.

"Nice game Greg, you had him," Jim stated and started to depart for his hotel room.

"No it wasn't," he heard Terry's choked up voice. "He was lucky. That wouldn't happen again in 99 more games."

Greg ignored the comment, Jim just shook his head in disgust, his nerves bothered him too much and the time had come to go get some food with Walters and relax for the next match. '*Walter's will get him,*' he thought walking away and didn't look back.

✳   ✳   ✳   ✳

The tournament continued in high fashion as the top four players swept the second round. The Dillards had some tough games, but proved to be far too strong in the endgame, while Walters and Jim just cruised to easy victories. Before supper they looked at the pairings and noticed an unusual amount of draws this round.

"Maybe five rounds will produce a single winner now," Walters commented about the inadequacies of the Swiss pairing system.

The two got in Jim's Mustang and headed for a local mall. The first place they sought out was a small Chinese buffet and they got in line to order their food. After grabbing their tray with two sesame chicken entrees with fried rice, they next went over to the ice cream stand and ordered up large strawberry smoothies, their favorite snack from years ago. Stacked with their scrumptious foods, they sat down and ate like kings.

"Gosh, I haven't had one of these in years," exclaimed Walters as he hammered his smoothie.

"This chicken is better than we make at the college," Jim replied, shoveling more food in his mouth. He could barely talk he ate so fast.

After ordering seconds on the rice and chicken, and getting yet another smoothie, the two decided that a short walk might help them process the big dinner and keep them a little sharper for the all enduring third round. They had played many hours of chess already today, and the next round only meant that they'd keep on playing tough opponents that also had not been beaten yet so far in the day. The opponents wouldn't be either of the Dillards yet, with them being at the top also, a showdown would certainly become apparent should they all keep on winning.

The two returned and checked their pairings. Jim had noticed he was paired against a high school kid that was up and coming, while Walters got paired against a long time former amateur champion. This type of pairing always held danger, because one never knew when a former champion of any sorts would decide to turn the chess strength on. He looked at Greg's name, and noticed the young player had won his earlier second round game, but his opponent also was a beginner.

Round three began and it proved to be an easy one for Jim. He ran through his inexperienced opponent ridiculously fast and even spent some time helping the young man improve his opening in the skittles room, where a few boards sat and people were allowed talk. After a warm handshake, he had made a new friend, but he treaded back to the tournament room to check on Walter's game.

Dismayed after learning Walters held a bad position, he started to calculate to see if a defense lay hidden somewhere deep in the complications. Again and again, he analyzed the game, while Walters paid him no mind. The big man sat with his chin on his fists and concentrated with full force on the game.

'Ah, there it is,' Jim toned to himself, '*it's almost 16 moves deep, and dang difficult to find.*' He examined the position deeper and realized a clever trap he didn't see earlier. '*Hmmm, at about the eighth move there is a crossroads. If he plays it perfect the one way, Walters can win the way I had seen. If he plays it the other way, it'll be a heck of a difficult battle, but he can save losing and get a draw. Anything else and he's toast.*'

He continued to talk to himself in his mind for quite awhile until Walters finally made a move. Like glue he stayed at the board, and slowly Walters followed the variation Jim had mapped until it came to the critical eighth move. Jim's nerves nearly made him keel over, and Walter's time started to get short. The game had progressed to its fifth hour and he wouldn't be able to take much more of this mental stress.

'The knight Walters, the knight,' he talked more in his mind, somehow hoping to maybe spread the idea via ESP. *'Not rook to c6, the knight, you can win this, not draw,'* he continued with his mental frenzy.

Walters didn't budge, he only had one move to make until time control and as long as at least one second remained on the clock, he'd use it to think his way out of this bad position. Finally, with the little red flag starting to teeter, he picked up the rook and slammed it down on the c6 square. Jim gasped in depression and went back to the room. He knew Walter's game would go at least two more hours now and he just couldn't handle watching anymore.

Leaving the tournament hall, he noticed Greg sitting in deep thought. He considered checking Greg's game out to see what kind of battle raged on his board, but declined, as he'd probably get stuck with more nerves watching that game too. He wondered how the heck he let Walters talk him into this whole affair. Matters seemed too uptight and now with his partner fighting for a mere draw, that left him all alone at the top with the Dillards.

Morning came soon enough and the I.H.O.P. again had been chosen as the favorite breakfast spot. They didn't talk about Walter's draw. Walters refused it every time it came up and didn't even care to see where he missed the win. They just filled their bellies with juicy bacon, sausage and gourmet pancakes with tangy rich syrup.

"I could feel it was a win," Walters finally acknowledged while completing his breakfast with a swig of fresh ice-cold milk. "I just got lost in one complication and didn't have the time to analyze everything."

"Well, you still can take four and a half. The guy didn't beat you."

"Berzchak, I'll do what I can to beat some of the top players, maybe even come in second." He finished his milk. "You though, can win this thing. You won't get a Dillard this morning there are six people left undefeated."

"But, I'll get one in round five."

"Yeah, and it'll be Dillard Senior and even if little Dillard goes undefeated as well to tie you for first, you are sure to beat him in tie-breaks."

"Well, first things first, I have to win round four and you know I have round five problems."

"Bah, I don't want to hear about round five problems. You're playing the best chess in your life Berzchak, maybe even in the whole state right now. You'll be fine."

"Yeah," Jim felt like arguing and then declined. His nerves gave him a twinge of grief. "Like I said, I have to win round four first."

"True," Walters replied and looked at his watch. "Hey, we better get going, it starts soon enough.

The two returned to the playing site and checked the pairing boards. Sure enough, one, two, three he and the Dillards had been matched against their opponents. Jim's opponent happened to be another former nemesis from high school, none other than the obnoxious Nate Knudson.

"One more board closer to ya dad," he heard Terry's annoying voice pipe. "When that other Esky guy loses, it'll be me and you in a tie for first."

"Son," Dillard Senior said and laughed an uneasy fake laugh. His nose lifted in the air some and the twinkle in his eye clearly showed over abundant admiration for his son. "I don't doubt it will, just take it easy."

Jim ignored the ludicrous prophecy and checked the standings page to see that Greg had scored another point in last night's game. This impressed him because most beginners lost all their games badly in their first tournaments. This blue-eyed blonde kid though, not only went toe to toe with Terry Dillard, he now had a couple ones in the win column and gained a tie for first in the unrated class.

At the board Jim set up his clock. He no sooner got settled and looked up to see a tall thin man with a scraggy beard and greasy ponytail.

"Nate," Jim quietly greeted.

"I'm not using that dumb antique," Nate replied, his face pale white with pockmarks. "We use digital clocks now, not that analog junk."

Annoyed Jim nodded and took 'Ticker' down and put it in his bag, while Nate replaced the empty spot with a beautiful high tech digital chess clock. The thing was the best money could buy and Jim recognized that it didn't even have plungers, but rather electric impulse sensors for making a move that worked much like a touch lamp.

"I see you haven't gotten any better since high school. Look, I'm not that far behind you now," Nate bragged.

"You're doing quite well," Jim replied in a nice and calm manner. Even though he felt otherwise he certainly had confidence against this player. The tournament director gave the go ahead to start and Jim offered his hand.

"Good luck."

"Oh you're going to need more than luck Berzchak," the wiry player said while he squeezed on Jim's hand. "Today you're mine," he released the handshake, touched the clock and it began to count down the time.

Another punk, Jim thought as he pulled his sweaty hand back. He had the white pieces and deliberately decided to wait 30 minutes before making his first move. He remembered reading about a grandmaster doing this in the past against a cagey and bothersome opponent. Today seemed like an excellent time to execute this great psychological strategy.

After ten minutes Nate started to get restless and after twenty he appeared beside himself seething inside with anger. To kill the time, Jim reminisced about the six different matches he and Nate had played in high school. Jim had never lost to Nate, but in four of the games Nate blew strictly won positions. The last time being the worst in that Jim had dropped his queen early with an extremely clumsy blunder. Yet, he hung on and it didn't take all that long before he managed to trap the opposing queen back in a fancy tactic. Nate wore his anger on his sleeve and this is what Jim did not like about the guy. He flew off the handle way too easy and acted so immature. Today, Jim knew this and totally used the fact to his advantage. The 30th minute finally elapsed and Jim played his first move, a pawn to e4.

Flustered Nate played his king pawn forward. Jim replied quickly and so did his opponent. Faster and faster Jim replied, but calculated everything sharply in his mind, while Nate stared him down in the duel. Eyes piercing on Jim he replied by slamming a captured piece on the digital clock. The clock refused to accept the move.

"Oh, that's a digital touch clock," Jim whispered. "You have to touch it with your finger, not with a piece like you can do on one of those junky analog clocks."

"Yeah, yeah, I know."

Feeling the insult and a little embarrassed, Nate's anger seemed to drop dramatically. Jim made another fast move and as expected, came a quick reply that turned out to be a serious mistake. Jim stopped his rapid play and started to mull the advantage now, while the opponent grimaced in mental anguish as to how he could be so dumb to get sucked into playing blitz like that. Jim took another half hour to make his next move, however, this time it was correct in doing so because he had to realize his big advantage. He made his next move nice and slow, tapped his clock and waited for the reply.

Nate sat for an hour, trying to find anything he could. After the long think, he knew he would lose a piece at best. Instead of fighting out a lost position, Nate tipped his king over and offered his hand to Jim.

"You didn't have to beat me so easy," he acknowledged in dismay. "One of these days Berzchak, I'm going to beat you."

"Thanks."

"Do me a favor though, and beat that chumpy kid or his dad. I'm the only real eccentric chess player around here and I don't feel like sharing."

"I'll try my best," Jim replied and laughed a nervous laugh.

CHAPTER 4

▼

A FIRST PLACE TIE

The final round had only three undefeated players left, the two Dillards and Jim. All three remained eligible to take clear first. Winning with a brilliant combination in his last game Walters held onto the fourth spot with slight chances at tying for the championship.

The final pairings set Jim against Dillard Senior and Walters matched against the son. The two Esky players knew this information long before the pairings had even been made and both decided to rest in the hotel room as long as possible before starting the grueling pace that the fifth round would demand.

Jim's head swirled in fatigue and he kept the pillow over it on the bed to relax. He had felt a headache coming on earlier and wisely took some ibuprofen to dull the throbbing. Though the pain had greatly diminished, he seemed to sense a tiring spell of confusion that he just couldn't shake to free his mind from the clouds.

"We're going shopping for a house tomorrow," Walters stated as a matter of fact.

"What?" Jim asked in surprise, taking the pillow off his head. "Why?"

Walters had also lain down on his bed to catch some needed mental rest, but his mind toiled over guilt for his friend's livelihood and financial arrangement. He wanted to help somehow.

"Remember when we always used to go fishing down at Ludington Park? Remember how we'd catch bass, pike and perch, sometimes even walleyes."

"Yeah."

"Well," he muttered trying to explain his guilt without making his friend feel like a charity case. "I want to do that again. I'm going to be out of the country for some time, but I know some pretty savvy finance people and they are always buying houses. Especially waterfront, they say you cannot lose. If I bought a house, would you go in on it with me? That way we'll get to fish again in the future."

Jim couldn't answer right away, however he noted his nerves were calm as could be. He loved fishing with Walters, cherished every second of it and just didn't have the time to go alone. His dream was to someday own a house on a lake if the finances ever improved. Working for the college though just didn't provide enough for him to buy a small house in town, let alone lakefront property. His mind wandered and then edged.

"I don't think I can afford that, it was a great idea Walters. You know we both love fishing almost as much as chess."

"Ah, but I think you might be able to," Walters interjected. "I can come up with a substantial down payment. I get my promotional 15 year officer's bonus in a couple months, I also have other monies that can be used." He sat up on the bed and looked Jim in the eye. "Let's do it, let's get a house. I'd need a good tenant to make this work anyway, so you can have a reduced living instead and also take care of the thing at the same time. You remember how much fun we had swimming, playing volleyball and practicing chess at Ludington Park before I left for the Navy. Remember that weather and the fun."

"The beer," Jim laughed, "even a girl's attention once in awhile."

"Let's do it."

Normally happiness beyond belief would have had Jim jumping for joy. Yet, inner fear sort of bit back at him. Something inside told him to proceed, the deal would be safe and he would do it, but his gut feeling also warned him something about the deal just didn't seem fair to Walters.

"All right Walters, let's do the math tomorrow and take a look at places on Lakeshore Drive." Jim agreed with prudence. "I put up my car though to help pay for it. Guy at work has a cheap one I can fix up. I get to help pay for this thing."

"Well, we'll see," he replied, but no way would he ever let Jim sell that beautiful car. He had a solid garage in mind for keeping that toy in magnificent shape. "Oh, one more thing," Walters remembered with concern. "I have something for you down the road. Right now isn't the best to talk about it and I've been saving it for a long time. I won't be able to get it for awhile, it's in a military storage shed in Florida," he laughed, "but someday you'll be surprised."

"Come on," Jim replied nervously, "what is it?"

"Nah, trust me, when you get it, it'll be a great surprise. You'll like it."

The two looked at the hotel clock and drew the conclusion that it was time to go down to the tournament room and take on their adversaries in the final round of competition. They gave each other a firm handshake like they used to do so many years ago and then put their fists together in a soft motion.

"You know what to do," Walters said, "time to rip them apart."

"Rip-apart," Jim mentioned their old magic phrase. His head still clogged with mental fatigue and confusion. He didn't feel good at all, but added, "I'll do my best."

In the tournament room, both Dillards sat side-by-side; ready to take on the old Esky players in a chess battle they felt would go to the bitter end. Walters sat down and extended his hand. At first the young opponent refused to oblige, until he saw an uncomfortable scowl on his father's face and decided to offer a limp shake to keep the situation peaceful. Jim and Dillard Senior also shook hands and after a lengthy final announcement by the tournament director all the game clocks in the room started in a rhythmic cadence. The final round had started and the last leg of the championship was upon them.

Walters seemed calm and moved his pieces with confidence. He sipped on a bottle of water. Jim glanced over at the position several times and the game already appeared to be a complicated mess created by two extremely skilled players. At the same time, he could not focus at all on his own game. The mental board in his mind remained blurry and concentration didn't exist. The only fortunate matter was that he and his opponent played 21 consecutive book moves of the Najdorf Variation from the Sicilian Defense that required no thinking whatsoever.

With the game progressing so much from memory, Jim used the extra time to get up and take a break. Dillard Senior knowing the position just as well took his extra time to watch the interesting position of his son's game. Jim walked out the door to the hotel lobby and just sat for an hour on a couch. He had a decision to make in his game and although frustrated his mental board still wouldn't come clear, analysis wouldn't be needed. Instead it all came down to a certain choice of move, much like a fork in a road.

'Do I play defensive or aggressive?' he thought. 'What would Walters want me to do? Well I know that, aggressive. I just don't know if I can beat Dillard Senior without being able to concentrate. Darn this round five stuff.'

On and on he rationalized, it was the only form of thinking he could manage. His nerves stayed calm but only because he knew deep down in his heart, he couldn't beat his opponent in this kind of mental shape. After a cup of coffee all by himself, he decided on playing a defensive line to steer the game into a quiet phase. He knew his chances of winning would be extremely low, but his chances of losing would be just as low. Survival without loss seemed to be his best course. '*Walters is going to kill me*,' he talked more to himself. '*Just do your best.*'

He returned to his game and made a quick move. Dillard Senior had an instant reply and the two followed ten more moves that mirrored a famous game played by Grandmasters Karpov and Kasparov. The two resembled encyclopedias more than actual thinkers. Jim knew this was his only chance. Without being able to concentrate, he had to use his last resource, his knowledge. He remembered a small trap he had discovered at home analyzing the position some time ago that could come up if the direction of the game continued. Four more exact moves of the game were played, Jim's nerves started to twinge. A little concentration came back and he didn't feel sure about the trap. A quick glance at Walter's deadlocked game told him he needed to finish as soon as possible. The trap held deep intricacies and refutations, maybe the elder Dillard would stumble.

In his chair he shook back and forth, still not able to concentrate fully, but totally remembering the trap, move for move. He glanced at 'Ticker' and saw it running down to 5 minutes left. Now he regretted taking such a long break earlier, he had to perform something quick and his whole plan of defense just reversed itself, this was as aggressive as chess could get. Finally, he decided to spring the trap and he fired his knight over to g5 setting the bait.

Dillard Senior grunted at the move. His face clearly showed that he did not foresee this move coming and he dug in to analyze the position. This took a lot of time and Jim's concentration started to break through the clouds and began to work again in spurts. His mental board shuffled pieces around and he could calculate the position again. Joy took him and could see things through and concentrate. With his strength back, winning became an option again.

Above his glasses with his head down, Dillard Senior eyed Jim's enthusiasm. His experience told him this move held extreme danger and although impressed because he couldn't see the right answer he had the edge to be a difficult opponent still. He looked at Jim's clock and noticed the low time and called upon his experience to decide an unexpected neutral move. Not accepting the trap, not refuting it either, he decided to do something different to make Jim think. He moved his pawn forward and pushed the button on top of 'Ticker'.

Jim hadn't even analyzed the move and looked stunned as Dillard Senior set his own sort of trap. He knew the move couldn't be any good and that there must be some sort of advantage to be gained. However, at times one needed an hour to find such subtle ways to defeat a high caliber player. To make matters worse, his focus betrayed him and disappeared. Instinct was all he had left again and he fired a move and heard Walters groan in dismay. He looked over at Walters, who returned a shrug and a headshake, only to return to his own clash.

He looked back at Dillard Senior who smiled and made another fast move. Move after move he sought to run Jim out of time. While each precious second ticked away, Jim's advantage on the board started to grow. Dillard Senior's strategy seemed to be backfiring. Jim clearly held a stronger game in this rapid style of making moves. Noticing this, Dillard Senior slowed down for a think and tried to regroup. Jim noticed Walters looking at his game again and his leg slightly shook left and right. Walters made eye contact and jerked his head and then Jim remembered their secret code that if one player saw a win for the other, they'd shake their leg back and forth and make eye contact.

Nerves really took Jim over and he couldn't move. Walters saw a win, but he couldn't see anything. Blindness was all he had and he couldn't get his mind to work. Only raw obvious moves were all he could manage. Finally Dillard Senior made a move and looked squarely at Jim.

"I'll offer a draw," Dillard Senior said sternly. He could see his game was lost, but decided to not force the issue of defeat if he didn't have to.

The words caught Terry's attention and he looked at his father's game with surprise. If that game ended a tie, and he could beat Walters, he could win the tournament outright himself.

With only a minute left Jim tried to think, but knew he couldn't overcome this mental deficit. He saw the win now, but it would take at least 25 moves to properly execute and it would be no secret that Dillard Senior would intentionally set traps to try for some weird error due to the time shortage. Two seconds a move normally would be enough time, but against a strong master and horrible fatigue, it just seemed impossible. No use losing the game on time when a draw would be assured.

"Okay," Jim replied and stopped the clock. "You're beat, but…"

"But you don't have any time," Dillard Senior coolly replied and Jim nodded in agreement.

Walters stamped his foot and then sat back down and continued with his own game. Fury took him and his face turned red with anger. Instead of getting bent out of shape though, he channeled the energy to his game. A tie for first place was now within his grasp. He knew his opponent's score as well and no way would he let this little brat win the tournament all by himself.

The pressure hit Jim at last and he couldn't watch any more chess. He went back to the lobby and quietly waited on a couch. After summing the scores in his head of Dillard Senior's opponents, Walter's if he won, and his own, he realized that Dillard Senior would win the 2004 Michigan Open title and first place trophy on tie-breaks. The result didn't surprise him.

Two hours had passed and at last Walters came out of the tournament room holding his score sheet, happy but not smiling.

"You win?" Jim asked.

"How did you blow that game? You had a win on that board at least three different times," Walters argued. "Why didn't you play it out? You're great at blitz, he was beat."

Jim shrugged. He felt his eyes get heavy with moisture, almost to the point of tears. His nerves turned to hurtful anguish and he did everything he could not to cry. He couldn't reply.

"Well, I beat that kid," Walters backed off and pumped out some good news. "The big Dillard wins the championship on tie breaks. You got second. I got third. As predicted somewhat I guess."

Jim nodded.

"Let's get our cash, I think it's like around $250 each," Walters mulled and rubbed his fingers together. "How about a steak dinner? I'll buy."

Jim nodded again. His mood started to pick up until he saw the Dillards come out of the tournament room with a big trophy. Terry's loss was not even noticeable. As long as his father took first his eyes showed approval.

"You guys blew it," Terry laughed while his father gave a slight smile and held up the first place trophy. "My dad told me all about your problems, can't win the big game?"

Emotions flooded from Jim's face and the tears welled in his eyes again. Walters gave him a nod to ignore them, but they continued to quietly laugh and admire their achievement. The act became a little ridiculous and Walters set off to tell them to get rid of their annoying antics, but stopped in his place and looked up as Ole Cookie and Greg approached them.

"Why don't you two goofballs make yourself useful and take a very long hike," Ole Cookie's voice boomed like a drum and scattered the Dillards right out of the lobby.

Embarrassed, Jim wiped his partial tears away before the others could see them and gave a smile. Walters patted him on the back to get going for steak, but Greg stood cautiously in front of them. Jim could tell the young man somehow understood his problems.

"Mr. Berzchak," Greg said calmly, "if you train me to play chess, I'll take them on, all of them. Win, lose or draw, no regrets."

The four of them remained silent for at least a minute.

"No regrets," Walter's broke the trance and tossed in his automatic support. He felt this type of activity could only help Jim. "A chess team right?" he added.

Greg nodded.

"No regrets then," Jim approved nodding his head with a sniffle. "You guys want to come have a steak dinner with us?" he offered. "We just tied for first place in the state's biggest open chess tournament."

"Guys," Ole Cookie kicked in and put his arm around his son. "The meal is on us—Greg here won the unrated section with three wins and won a hundred bucks himself. I am mighty fine proud of him."

Jim and Walters exchanged surprised looks and smiled. Both their minds held the same question, 'Is this kid a real chess-player?'

CHAPTER 5

▼

HOUSE ON A LAKE

A light orange sunrise above the water from Lake Michigan captured Jim's sight as he stood on the deck of the new house. All summer Walters had brokered the deal from his new command on the U.S.S. Riddick Sea. He used satellite internet and faxes like a madman from the ship's resources and did a wonderful job getting the house from $330,000 in asking price to $300,000 complete with all closing costs, appliances, some furniture and toys such as the boat and dock. This house had been the only one they looked at before he left the United States and he knew the minute Jim walked into it that this was the one they had to have.

Difficult as it had been to bargain with the previous owners, he lobbied for this investment and their dream. He did have to drain his whole IRA plus throw in his officer's bonus check to pay it off in cash. Yet, his financial people gave him the go ahead on the deal since he had no children, a good chunk of his savings still in the bank and a fabulous military pension coming in the next five years regardless of how this investment went. He had set himself up for life through a strict lifestyle of discipline and now the time had come for a pay off.

The financial people did not know however that the renter wouldn't be providing significant cash income. In fact, he insisted both of their names appear on the deed, a definite financial taboo or no-no. The move held extreme risk and at the same time it offered a unique protection to each of them. The arrangement had been built on trust and not just any two friends could get away with such a big partnership. The two held a bond of brotherhood and if he couldn't trust

Jim, he couldn't trust anyone. Even if he did get married some day and had ten kids, Jim would still be in his life and probably teaching all those kids to play chess no doubt. The deal was for Jim's best interest anyway. This would be the start of a calmer, healthier, less harsh lifestyle for him. Neither of them would do anything to jeopardize their friendship. From that point on Walters refused to give the matter of trust any further concern. They both owned the house and he had peace with that.

Jim winced when he tried to comprehend such numbers a house on Lakeshore Drive like this cost. He also remembered Walters telling him though that the price could be considered a steal compared to other places in the country and the investment portion was a guaranteed winner. After getting up from that first night's rest, he couldn't recall getting a better sleep anywhere. The move a day earlier was simple, only three loads of clothes, one load of junk, a computer and one big box of chess equipment and books that he easily hauled in his car.

Again and again he checked out the house in disbelief that he really had permission to live there. The house had three bedrooms, three bathrooms, a den, large kitchen, family room, fireplace and a connected two-door garage to die for. He checked on his car quick and couldn't resist a smile as it sat protected from the elements on a clean concrete floor.

Back inside he looked at all the bedrooms once again, for the amusing reason that he could and then went to his bedroom. The choice of bedrooms the day before had taken him a little while to make. The master bedroom certainly had great size and elegance. The green bedroom had unique architecture and superb decoration. The blue bedroom had its own bathroom and large closet. In the end, he chose the blue room because it offered the most aesthetic view of the lake, something he wanted to indulge in as frequent as possible.

After the newness had worn off a little, he went to the den and unpacked his chess gear. Walters had a beautiful oak chess table that his sister had brought the night before and he decided to make this area the new chess headquarters. This would be where all his main chess research and practice activity would take place. Alongside the table sat a wooden computer desk that the previous owners had left. The desk sat like a letter 'L' in the room. He moved the oak table next to the desk and set up the board. Next he plugged in all the wires to his computer and the area began to hum with activity. Last came his chess books and he stacked all 104 of them on the bookshelves that were built right into the wall.

"Walters is going to love this," he exclaimed about the three empty shelves that awaited more books.

With most of the day's chores completed, hunger rumbled in his belly. A meal of pan-fried fish came to his mind first. He had already bought some bread coating in a box and a few potatoes. In anticipation of this moment, he also picked up a few extra lures and a box of leaf worms for bait the day before. Fishing would not be delayed any longer.

The weather outside was gorgeous and he strolled to the dock. The previous owners had left it in place as requested. If he needed to he could easily pull out the 14-foot boat and motor combo for a ride in deeper water and bigger excursions. But, the calm day just didn't hit him with the need to go far and instead he decided to stay in and enjoy shore fishing. He hauled a lawn chair out on the dock along with a cool glass of lemonade and made another trip to get his rod and reel. As he sat back in the chair waiting for a bite, he felt the morning breeze across his face and how it could not be more perfect and then he relaxed. In a short time the fish started to bite and he landed one big perch after another.

"Boy, these are going to be good," he commented to himself, amazed at the nice catch.

He caught several more, enough for lunch and looked up into the sky. He said a small prayer of thanks for all his recent good fortunes and another that Walters would be safe during the dangerous missions on his ship touring the Persian Gulf.

Inside the house he cleaned his catch, breaded the fresh fish fillets and heated up a frying pan of oil. The fillets sizzled when he set them in the pan and he periodically rotated them with two forks so they would not burn. After finishing the first batch, he seasoned the next fillets and stuck a couple potatoes in the microwave.

The completed meal filled the house with a distinct cooking odor. While many people didn't care for the strong smell, he loved it. The meal dazzled his taste buds and he crammed his belly full of the yummy fish. '*Brain food*,' he thought and forced himself not to waste a bite.

He looked at the clock and realized he had a few spare hours to rest before his short shift at work, so he retired to his room. A cool and comfortable breeze with a twinge of lake smell pushed through the bedroom window. His soul felt at peace and his nerves had never been calmer. He slept well.

The rest did not last long and Jim's work shift at the college cafeteria was due to begin soon. Cleaning up in the bathroom he reflected upon his schedule and how it worked. He had two types of workdays, the long ten-hour workday and the short six-hour workday. These shifts staggered to give him full time employment status with benefits and the minimum biweekly 64 hours the job required. He really liked the schedule and today happened to be a six-hour shift.

He particularly enjoyed the six-hour days during summer because Ole Cookie would bring Greg over after the place closed for business and they would sit in the bright and comfortable lighting of the cafeteria and practice chess. Ole Cookie would sometimes help Jim with cleanup so he could spend more time on the game with Greg.

For three months they had been working on Greg's game a little bit here and a little bit there. The mutual friendship grew even further and Jim started to trust and be more comfortable around the young player. However, Greg needed a tremendous amount of work on his game yet. For only being a sophomore in high school he had quite a lot to learn in order to be competitive with the state's best players. He could think back to how he'd clearly overpower Greg when he was the same age.

The boy did possess an inner strength that couldn't be explained and that Jim had not admired in anyone else. This kid could fight at the board with awesome tenacity and although he didn't have the weapon chest of tactics and strategy a strong player would have, he definitely made up for it in determination and sure will power.

Even after the practice sessions, Greg's face would flush red from effort. He wanted to be at Jim's winning level now or at least beat him just one time. Jim noticed this drive and actually did a good job in tempering the overachievement plea. The key to mastery of chess was to grind out basic principles on a frequent basis, much like planting a tree and watering it daily. The process took time, energy and care and at the same time it could bring immense fatigue, distracting boredom and horrible frustration. If followed correctly, growth of a good chess player would take place in tiny increments and if lucky every once in awhile a large spurt forward could be made. One could not wish to be a strong master in just a couple of months. Even the teenage grandmasters of the time had to put thousands and thousands of hours of practice into the game. Sure, they were gifted all the same, but even the most genius of geniuses had to pay their dues of working hard in order to succeed and get better at chess.

"Why can't I beat you Mr. Berzchak?" Greg asked. He toppled over his king in resignation.

"Ah, ah, ah, never resign," Jim contested, "you know the rule."

"Why can't I just resign and start a new battle?" Greg picked his king back up. "Something that means something."

"Someday I'll tell you why. For now, just don't do it all right?" Jim lectured with a calm voice and a small grin that had the makings of a smile. "Believe me, it makes sense."

The two continued to play out the hopelessly lost position. A couple moves had gone by and Greg realized a neat fighting position, albeit lost, did arise and his teacher's words seemed somewhat true now. At last Jim's forces surrounded Greg's king and forced the monarch into submission.

"When are we going to start a team?" Greg asked politely.

"Probably during the school year."

"I know that," Greg laughed, "but when?"

"Oh," Jim realized his error. "We always used to start in October. How about then? I still need to get permission from the school and get a room and of course, tell them I'm volunteering and that we'll fundraise any expenses we need."

"How about in September?" Greg countered.

"I don't know, maybe. Did your dad get those chess books ordered?"

Ole Cookie heard the question and walked over to them pushing his broom.

"You bet I did," Ole Cookie's voice commanded. "One hundred bucks worth. I hope they're good Berzchak, you're costing me a fortune."

The materials were actually quite good ones. Jim had compiled a small list of the best chess books he had ever read. Greg made out like a bandit in terms of efficiency because he would get the good ones right away, the lessons in them would be systematic and it gave him a clear direction of study for improvement.

"Cookie," Jim said. His nerves felt a little askew. He wasn't sure he should ask, but decided to anyway. "Would you possibly be interested in being my assistant coach?"

Father and son looked at each other in surprise and Greg's face lit up with a smile and a nod. Most high school boys didn't want their parents around for anything. For Greg, since his mom had deserted them to live with another man in New Mexico, this parent-child combination with his dad resembled one more like best friends with minor limitations.

"Sure," Ole Cookie piped with a wide smile that bared his coffee stained teeth. "Can't say I can help you too much though, Greg's a lot better at chess than I am and you know how busy we get here at work. I'll try the best I can though even if my help is only minimal."

"Well, I can cover the game itself Cookie, I sort of need an extra chaperone and maybe help driving. Things like that," Jim's nerves flared, he wasn't sure if he had offended the strong man. "I mean, I don't mean it like you're not good at chess or anything like that."

"I know what you mean," Ole Cookie replied firmly, "and yes, I'd be honored to help. That's if Greg here doesn't mind."

"I do-not-mind, thanks dad," Greg chimed in a positive tone and looked at Jim. "Thanks Mr. B. You don't mind if I call you that do you?"

"Not at all, I actually think that's a lot easier," Jim reassured. "Okay, that settles it. We will start our chess club and chess team the last week of September."

Jim could barely walk he shook from nerves so bad. At the same time he couldn't be more pleased than to have a fairly strong 10th grade high school player to start the year with and an assistant coach as tough as nails to help him with technicalities. These two were fine. They could be trusted. The only problem that seemed to remain was who the heck else would show up for this future chess team?

CHAPTER 6

▼

THE ESCANABA ESKIMOS

A skilled chess player never made a move without having some sort of plan or goal in mind first. Far too often the rank amateur flat out did what he felt like doing because he based all his decisions on mere emotion and didn't pay attention to details. The amateur's way lead to errors and Jim knew this also applied in coaching. He had to have a good plan for his first year as a chess coach. A lot would have to be done and they didn't even have any pieces or boards to play on.

Sure, from past experience and tradition, club would be held on Tuesday nights from 6 to 8 in the biology rooms if possible. The team would consist of at least four players, but for the most part the sessions would be open to as many players as he could get to join. More he felt though, needed to go into a solid working frame in order to get the kids to a competitive level.

'How about two nights a week?' he thought to himself. *'Can they handle that?'*

One thing he really regretted from his own high school days was not taking advantage more of a coach that would put in the time. Many times his old coach offered the extra day and many times the players rested on their laurels. They had excellent firepower and good work ethics, some of the best around and at the same time they turned down golden opportunities to work even harder. That wouldn't happen again. This time he'd start the team with two days of practice a week and nobody outside of himself would know the difference.

The schedule came to his mind next. If he started things on time, that left less than a month. What tournaments gave the best chances at quality experience?

How many team events should they attend? All these kinds of things had to be thought out and answered soon.

After pondering some ideas, the state team championships jumped out at him. Of course, this would be their building block goal. Being in a position to win the state title had to be the number one direction and all other goals had to be secondary. He didn't want to base this new team solely on winning alone. Instead he chose to look at it like having the question, "why are we here?" with the answer, "to play well and be in the position to have a reasonable chance to win a state championship."

He wanted good sportsmanship and for the game to be fun for these youngsters. Building new memories of excellent times for today's youth held great importance to the equation of his volunteering. The overall premise was one of being a productive person in society. All this held true and dear to his heart. He even felt good thinking about it and still every mental road he traveled about the whole situation led to winning that elusive state title.

'It's okay to want to win,' he pictured Walters lecturing to him. 'As long as you do a good job, promote the proper ethics, you're allowed to want to win. That is a fine goal.'

That had settled it; the chance at a title came first. There stood a thousand hurdles between this goal's achievement and 900 of them dealt with getting the club up and running. For the rest of the evening he jotted down a long outline of things to get done. He made a list of things to do and even constructed the club's first announcement poster. He badly wanted to print it with a starting date and decided to keep calm and refrain until all the details had been finalized.

'Make sure you do things right and think them out,' the Walters in his mind told him.

"I will," Jim replied smiling at the poster. "Don't worry, they'll be in good hands."

Four weeks of hard work brought the first night's long awaited arrival. After all the permission had been granted and all the details cared for, Jim had finally got things ready for the first night. A half an hour early he entered the same biology room that he had played in during his own school days. A moment of silence took him and the good memories almost brought a tear to his cheek. A feeling of peace owned the room and he promised to do his best to keep that perception alive and well for the next generation of chess players. His nerves panged a little with fear. They also shook him up with some excitement.

He had brought four cheap sets with him that he purchased earlier in the afternoon from the store. The sets didn't hold much value and they looked kind of weird on their red and black checker backgrounds. Future fundraising would enable the club to get nice weighted Staunton pieces along with roll-up vinyl boards, the same sets used in sanctioned tournaments. Tonight however, just having something to play on was good enough.

Not long after Greg and Ole Cookie showed up. Even though they were quite close in friendship, they shook hands. Behind them came a couple of other sophomore students Greg seemed to know well.

Refusing to use the cheap sets, Greg set up his regulation sized board and pieces and started to play. A couple more students showed up and Jim felt relieved to get five players. Only four players made up a team, but having that extra player always meant good things in terms of insurance. Jim studied the group while waiting for more players to arrive. He noticed Greg immediately take the leadership roll as he showed the others moves on his board.

The attendance seemed to halt as nobody else showed up for the club and Jim decided to get some chores out of the way. He introduced himself and had the players put their names, grade level and e-mail addresses on a sheet of paper. Next he made a few announcements regarding future activities and then asked for nominations of a club president, someone to help out at the student level. No surprises showed as Greg won the only nomination and took the election by default.

"Tonight guys I'd like to try and play you all a game and try to get a feel where everyone is at," Jim announced, his nerves unusually calm.

A tall heavyset kid stood up to take him on first. Although certainly overweight he exuded an air of confidence and strength, much like Walters, while at the same time held kindness in his personality.

"Hi I'm Alan Wilson," the young man stated and offered his large hand in greeting.

"Nice to meet you," Jim replied.

They took a seat at an open board and Alan moved his king rook pawn first. Jim replied with a solid central pawn move and Alan sat undecided staring at the position with his hand on his cheeks staring at the pieces with his dark brown eyes. After rubbing his nose a couple times, he made a very defensive move. Jim liked the fire in this kid's eyes. He had intensity much like Greg, only in a different softer-defensive style. The game battled on and Jim spread out his forces and soon collapsed Alan's king with a bombardment of knights and rooks.

"Not bad Alan," Jim said ending the game with checkmate. "You play extremely defensive chess."

"That's odd," Alan replied, "I thought I was more of an attacker."

"Well," the coach nodded, "you just like to set up for an attack first, and there is nothing wrong with that. There was a grandmaster long ago named Tigran Petrosian. He started off with super defensive positions." Jim noticed the young man listen with interest. "His plans a lot of times were to be like a rubber band. Pull back, defend, pull back, defend and just when everything is tight, release and snap right back at the opponent."

"Ah," Alan smiled, "I see what you mean."

"Most players that emulate Petrosian are tough to beat and they have some of the neatest positions that arise. Good game Alan, you're going to be a good one."

Jim could tell Alan felt good, and he enjoyed the excitement in Alan's eyes. He motioned to another player to join him and a student of medium build with his sandy blonde hair parted to the side sat at the board.

"Tyler Krockett," he stated and sat down.

"Nice to meet you Tyler, how long have you been playing?"

"Since I was in elementary school, but on and off," he said and wiped his hand over his hair. Jim could tell this young man had an excellent upbringing and a solid middle class family to back him up. No doubt this kid had parents behind him that knew how to do their parenting duties well. "My dad and I play a lot. I can never beat him. He's so good. One of these days I'd like to win just one game against him."

"Oh, I think we can do something about that," Jim said and moved a piece on the board. "If we do it right, we can even turn the tables on him for good."

Tyler sat with his hazel eyes locked onto the board. His opening moves were just horrible and Jim crushed him immediately in six moves.

"Good game Tyler—Don't let this discourage you, there is a lot to learn."

"Can you tell me what move I went wrong on?"

Surprised by the question, Jim lifted his eyebrows to give a solid explanation without making any hard feelings. "Well to be honest Tyler, you're second move was suspect. Pushing your f pawn prematurely like that can be quite devastating. I'll tell you what," Jim shuffled a couple pieces around. "Try this next time," he demonstrated a nice line and Tyler memorized it on the spot. He quickly set the pieces back up and went through the line again.

"Is this what you were talking about Mr. Berz—ch, I can't pronounce it."

"Go ahead and call me Mr. B and yep, you got it," Jim replied in amazement. "Do you have a photographic memory?"

Tyler smiled at the compliment, "Well no, it's pretty good though and I do read a lot and am pretty sharp in school."

"He's never had a grade lower than an A in school," Greg interrupted from across the table, "ever."

Tyler shook his head in embarrassment.

"Well done," Jim smiled. "In a couple weeks, when we get more settled, I'll show you a couple other lines and we can get down a solid opening system for you to play."

"Thanks," Tyler replied and he motioned to another kid at Greg's board, "Jeff you're turn."

Jim watched Jeff stand up. He had tall legs but a short torso. His face looked long and narrow and his nose mimicked that of a bird's beak. His ears each donned a diamond stud and his jeans had white wear marks from over use. The other kids didn't seem all that comfortable around him, but when speaking the language of chess most other things in life were forgivable.

"I'm gonna tear him apart," Jeff announced to the group and headed over to the chessboard.

"Hi Jeff nice to meet you," Jim offered a handshake and he noticed his insides had jumbled a bit.

With a goofy grin and beady black eyes that could pierce the soul he took Jim's hand by the fist and gave him a gang type of handshake. A little annoyed with the opening comment Jim decided to show the feisty player who would crush whom and set up a simple scholar's mate. Sure enough it worked and in four lightning quick moves the game ended and Jeff sat staring speechless.

"Whoa, dude," he finally spoke. "How did you do that?"

Jim started to calm down and backed the position up. "Now that you know the checkmate is coming, can you stop it?"

Jeff looked at the position for some time and then moved a pawn in front of his king.

"That's it, well done, that's the way to stop it. Most people can't find that the first time."

"Oh boy, am I ever going to destroy everyone with this trick."

"Well Jeff, I hate to burst your bubble, but that's all it is, is a trick. You can't rely on it." Jim cautioned. "Best to learn real play, trust me if you try that on me, I can stop it and then of course, make you pay for trying it."

"Yeah, but that's you. I can get everyone else."

Jim took a deep breath inside. The kid had a troubled appearance and a fiery personality to match. The mix could very well turn him into an excellent chess player if done right. He knew he'd have to double-time it with this one. Exceptional chess talent appeared to be in him naturally, but the behavior and manners, now that entailed a whole different strategy to making a great competitor.

The next player that came to Jim's board had a familiar look to his face and blue eyes. Just something about the dark red hair and husky build led him to believe he knew this boy from somewhere.

"Hi I'm Craig Bellington," the boy greeted.

The moment he heard the name Jim knew who he was. "You related to Brad Bellington?" he inquired of his old teammate.

"Sure am, he's my uncle. He taught me to play chess years ago. I'm not very good. I could make a good team manager though."

"Well, I'm sure there is a spot for you," Jim said hoping the boy had even an inkling of his uncle's chess strength. "How has your uncle been these days? Does he play anymore?"

"Nah, he'll play me if I ask him on vacation breaks when he comes to my grandma's for a visit. He is really into his career and just doesn't seem to have the time." Craig paused and broke eye contact with Jim. "He kind of has complained that chess wasn't worth the hassle in competition. He said to just have fun with it. Too much of a let down, he says don't get too serious about it."

The words poked at Jim like a needle and each one stung. He knew to remain strong though; he could weep about his friend's ill feelings later with his fishing pole on the dock. Now would be the time for strength and to get the past in the open.

"Yeah, what he means is I blew the state championship 15 years ago," Jim admitted keeping his face stern with fortitude. The whole room hushed and his words brought everyone to silence for a long pause.

"Do you think your uncle is still mad about it?" Jim asked. The others started to carry on again at the same time still listening.

"I don't think so. He said something about unfulfilled dreams due to a bad lapse, not mad or anything." Craig made eye contact again. "One thing he said was when I asked him last week on the phone about joining chess is that you were one of the best players he ever knew, someone that could be trusted."

"Thanks Craig," Jim nodded. "Wanna play a game?" he offered while the thoughts started to go away. Chess was the only quick cure for these uneasy emotions.

The two started to push pawns and pieces and Jim annihilated his young opponent. So much so, they played another game and the results were even worse the second time around. Dismay took him, the kid was correct. He held little or no talent at all and his moves seemed like he had just learned the rules an hour ago. Jim still smiled and bid him a good game.

"Not very good hey?" Craig asked while his heart sank. "Like I say, I can make a good team manager or something. I'd really like to be on the team somehow."

"Well I'll tell you what, if you keep working on your game and help me with some chess chores as they come, I'll make sure I have an alternate position. The team only needs four players, but we are allowed a fifth player that can substitute in, much like a backup quarterback in football. You'd officially be on the team and can partake in all the rights and privileges and of course have the same responsibilities as if you were a starter. You just won't get to play a lot until we get a chance to put some chess muscle on you. Does that sound fair enough?"

"It sure does Mr. B," Craig answered with relief.

The night quietly came to a close with Jim taking Greg down in a couple blitz games and then the club members went home. They smiled and chatted as they left and the feeling was one of good things to come. With the biology room empty he sat alone for a long while reflecting on Craig's words about his uncle. He felt horrible again, 15 years later for blowing that state title, but knew he'd have to try and get over it.

Despite the hurt of so long ago, he needed to move forward. His emotions wouldn't give up so easily though. This problem had not been solved. When the solutions of remedy appeared he ran away like a scared kitten. He looked over the boards and picked them up. This room held such an air of serenity to it he didn't want to leave. He knew now he'd have to try and deal with this problem, no matter how upset it made him feel. Some day he'd need to make amends somehow to his old teammates for blowing their championship run. If only he had stood up to this in the first place at the actual tournament and stood up for himself instead of letting it burn inside him for so many years.

This was the present now and the present led to the future. The mistake was in the past. The time had come to make some changes and get his life going forward again. The Escanaba Chess Team was back on its tracks. He smiled as he left, and whispered his team's old saying, "Eskychess Express is ready to roll."

CHAPTER 7

▼

LET THE PRACTICE BEGIN

The first few meetings Jim had the players square off in a double round robin club tournament with a time control of game in 60 minutes. 'Ticker' and a couple other old chess clocks he owned were used to accomplish the task until funds could be raised for new equipment. Most of the players loved to play blitz chess that only gave each side three to five minutes to complete their whole game. This made for some exciting play, but in a sanctioned tournament, opponents would not get drawn into playing fast or be tricked into easy mistakes. On the other hand a game couldn't go on all night either, so 60 minutes for each player made certain the game did not last more than two hours total all the while giving each player plenty of time to think and play a somewhat quality game.

When the smoke cleared Jim used the results to rank the players in order of strength and set his starters by these positions. Greg had gained a clear first place with all wins outside of an outrageous draw with Jeff in a complicated game that gave both players fits. Jeff placed second himself only losing one game against Greg and one against Tyler. Everybody felt tension during his game with Tyler when he almost tipped the board over in anger. Fortunately he thought better of the action and cursed quietly under his breath instead. Big Alan took third and Tyler held up the fourth board position. Last place went to Craig Bellington who lost every single game he played and worse yet he didn't even hold a competitive game against any of the other players.

For a lengthy time after the boards had been officially ranked the team worked on their game twice a week. Jim's confidence started to soar and he started to feel inner strength build inside his character. All signs of nerve problems began to diminish.

The players recognized him as a chess genius and in their eyes he looked like a ten foot tall giant full of muscles. He never lost a game to any of the players, but he still instructed them clearly on their mistakes and offered positive down to earth suggestions for improvement. They could ask him just about any question they could think of regarding chess and Jim always gave a clear and reasonable response. He knew nearly everything there was to know at their level and the group could easily see his love for the game. No virus could ever be as contagious as his enthusiasm.

His first action as coach was to declare the borrowed Flint rule of no resignation. He stated that under no circumstances would any player on his team resign. If a player did resign he had no clue what he'd do to handle it. Chess punishment didn't have the equivalent of wind sprints like a physical sport. Instead he stressed the rule verbally and in a convincing manner and that left the players to realize this rule.

"What if we're getting killed and there is no hope," Jeff argued. "What's the use, why humiliate us like that?"

Jim had a prepared reason on his tongue ready to use. "Because I blew a state championship when I had my opponent dead to rights 15 years ago." His face went to stone for a long moment of silence. Holding his anxiety in his gut, he continued, "I'm a skilled chess player and you think I'm pretty good at chess right? If I can mess up, it goes to speak that anyone can mess up right? You never know what will happen in a game of chess. I can't recall anyone in the chess history books who ever won a game when they resigned. Always remember the impossible can and sometimes will happen. Do not resign."

The team also worked hard on tactical methods. Jim's plan was to have the toughest chess team around and step one of this teaching plan had them focused totally on tactics. His players at the beginning level showed very green levels of newness. The workings were there, but even Greg had much more development at this point to achieve. In order to get them playing competitive fast, he repeated force fed chess tactics on them. He ordered chess books that contained thousands and thousands of chess puzzles in diagram format. Every week he provided a large dose of chess of these puzzles, which usually consisted of four easy diagrams, one medium problem and one hard one. The plan's path to mastery for these young players included daily chess exercises, much like a chess vitamin and he pounded this philosophy, week after week.

Surprisingly, the kids took the diagrams and improved tremendously. Only Jeff refused to go along with the program. Fortunately his chess strength still grew because he played so much chess on the internet at home and his club attendance was perfect. He certainly loved the game and loved to play. He also loved to win, but practice, that held a whole different perception to him and he couldn't be budged on it. Nevertheless, the rest of the team continued with assigned tactics, enjoyed them and after a couple of months stopped making simple mistakes altogether. They moved past the beginner stage and started to become quite strong junior chess players.

Even with all the hard work and long hours of enjoyable practice the team still had huge gaps in experience. The solution required a second phase to the teaching plan. Tactics were the easy part, due to the systematic methods involving logic and study. Strategy though, held a whole different mystique. Most if not all of these players would probably never reach a complete understanding of positional chess in their natural lifetimes. The thought seemed eerie to Jim because some advanced positional ideas he had learned in self-study took him 10 years to understand and that kind of time for the team did not exist. Sure, he could make a lot of short cuts and be there for the players to explain things well. At the same time after three years of solid study the players on the team still would not be able to hold a candle to him. He had a simple answer though for this breach in confidence and the answer was that he didn't need strong masters to have a good time on a chess trip or to win a state championship. A group of dedicated players that played their hearts out in a tough manner could satisfy any chess dilemma.

The third phase of his teaching plan involved psychology with confidence. He toiled over this horrible weakness that glared in his own games. How could he teach these kids to be tough mental monsters when he couldn't do it himself in a tournament? However, he decided to just be firm, lean on Ole Cookie's sleeve for support and manage his players with his heart. Ole Cookie could bark at the kids when they got into mischief and they certainly listened to him. Jim on the other hand decided the role of nurturer best suited him. He couldn't do this alone right now, not until he had more experience. He thanked the stars on many evenings while sitting on his dock at home that Ole Cookie could help him manage the behavior of the team, especially with Jeff who still seemed to make him nervous from time to time.

"We're going to be the toughest team," Jim would say at practice like a calm football coach and meant it while suppressing his own fear. If anyone not affiliated with the team had seen him act like this, they wouldn't recognize him, but the kids were learning to play chess well and at an incredible pace. They perceived none of his anxious quirks and viewed his personality as rather normal if not exceptional. "It doesn't matter if you win, lose or draw, as long as you are the toughest team. Take it to your opponent and if you get knocked down, get back up. If you lose, make your opponent remember how tough you were and that next time they're in for it again and again and again, until you conquer. I will teach you everything I can about chess. I'm willing to share and I have no problems of any of you getting better than me at chess. I don't want to be selfish here. In return, all I ask is that you play tough for me and we'll call it a fair deal."

As the weeks pressed on Jim seemed to get divine strength when it came to the team and even with Jeff's crazy mannerisms and foul mouth, he started to connect with the whole group. Good things one after another kept happening and by the third month, when even Craig solved a mate in three at practice without any help, he started to believe a championship run could be in order.

The plan had been set, the team started to bond and after a reassuring email from Walters, he knew this team had a chance. That chance came with a price and would be a tremendous long shot even in the best-case scenarios. To defeat a team like Flint with the likes of both Dillards running the show, took more work than any of the players could even comprehend at this point. Even the best-case scenarios required some sort of good fortune. If the players had any clue of the toil they had yet to endure, they may not jump on this ride. However, they didn't and this group was worth the investment and good fortune was not beneath them. A state team chess championship had a chance of happening.

Right before Christmas break; Jim went to work on getting some chess matches with other schools scheduled. A small chess league between four local schools, West Iron County, Negaunee, Gwinn and Marquette already existed and had a long history, way back even from when Jim played. With many phone calls, emails and some serious begging, he successfully restored Escanaba's old spot in the league and the schedule had been set for January and would conclude in early March before the state championships were held. He knew that for Upper Peninsula chess, his team could compete well. Even with owning a serious deficiency in tournament performance they might even contend or possibly win the weak league.

In the final stretch of the calendar year, the team started to become fatigued with playing each other in practice. They started to show signs of impatience from a long training regime. Here Jim decided to give them a break. He thought of the old saying, 'All work and no play makes Jack a dull boy.' He started to really understand the workings of his team and knew he couldn't press too much further without getting the positive effects of tournament experience under them first. So, he suspended all chess games between club members for the whole month of December until their school holiday break had concluded.

"What will we do?" Greg asked like he had to give up a good friend.

"Sell candles," Jim replied whipping out a flyer printed with lots of sales materials. "We need some cash because the school can provide nothing but a van for us to use, and even at that we have to pay the gasoline in travel. So we are going to earn our way to trips and buy some new fancy chess equipment."

"I'll do that," Big Alan stated, "but I also want to keep playing chess too."

"Don't worry, I'll keep your tactics homework coming and of course, you guys can play computer chess programs at home, just stop beating on each other, you're getting tired. We get Negaunee in the second week of January in our league and we need to start focusing on them and at the same time relieve the fatigue of practice. We just don't want to burn ourselves out gentlemen."

"Oh yeah, fresh meat," Jeff blurted with delight.

The rest of the team also seemed to like the idea of playing somebody fresh and new.

All five players managed to sell several hundred dollars in candles a week before Christmas. Jim had remembered that when he asked the superintendent for money earlier in the year, he was simply handed a flyer. He never dreamed such a boring task could be so profitable. "Instant money maker—Quality item," the superintendent told him and at the same time dismissed him so he didn't use up any more precious time.

The truth of the matter was that selling candles did turn out to be a winning activity. The players hated the idea of begging for sales and hustling so hard for what seemed like tiny scraps. However, they plugged away and sold as much as they could. When all the sales had been completed and all the orders filled, the club had over $500 dollars in their school savings account to use for whatever they wanted.

With the profits they decided first to order chess equipment and shirts. Tyler had unique artistic abilities and designed a logo for the team with an Eskimo sitting in an igloo leaning against a board studying a chess position with the phrase 'Esky-Chess' neatly curved over the top. Jim took the work to a local apparel store that easily transposed it with orange and black thread onto a flat white polo shirt. Each student chipped in a couple bucks to help subsidize the costs, while Jim paid cash for his. Satisfied with the large order, the company also personalized the shirts for each player at no added cost. When the project was completed, they tried on their shirts one Tuesday night and looked like a real team in uniform. The shirts were made of quality cotton and the team looked impressive. Jim looked down and read with pride 'COACH BERZCHAK' on his shoulder sleeve. Even in his day they never wore such nice uniform shirts.

After the shirts, Jim saved a hundred dollars for future gasoline expenses and spent the rest of the money on boards and pieces, several chess clocks, some positional books, a copy of Modern Chess Openings 14, score sheets and a few other chess knickknacks. He ordered so much, the company upgraded his shipping to express at no extra cost and the order arrived the last day before break. The team felt great joy and couldn't resist playing each other. With Christmas seeming to arrive early in a chess sense, Jim revoked the no playing rule for the day and they played for an extra long session on their brand new gear.

"See what hard work can buy guys?" Jim nodded with a smile. The team looked delighted and kept on with their games. "Guess what?" he asked and all the chess players stopped and looked at him. "We get to do another candle sale in January."

"Gosh no," Craig whined with the backing of his peers. "Please don't make us do that again."

"We could go to States, that's if you guys wanted to sell a few candles." Jim continued with a sneaky grin.

The players groaned a small groan and then lit up with smiles. The statement had duel meaning. Sure another laborious task of selling more darn candles, but also the coach's commitment to going to the state championship tournament. Their pride soared. Jim had done his duties well and the team was hungry to take on other teams in competitive chess.

"We have to learn firsthand what competition is like and it's not going to be easy. I can promise you that. It's a rough building process. You guys have done a wonderful job up to this point. I say we get ready to let some of these other teams feel how tough the Eskychess Express really is."

CHAPTER 8

▼

FIRST COMPETITION

Only one word described the team's mood in the van on the way to Negaunee for their first chess meet, 'intense'. The players barely managed to sleep the night before and complained about the school day dragging slowly. Jim even had them excused for the last two hours of class in order to make a gain on travel time and the team's day still went slow for them. During the ride Tyler produced a little magnetic chess set and much of the team hawked over it in practice the whole way.

Jim told the group many stories about his past experiences going to tournaments along with some celebrated anecdotes of previous Escanaba team members his coach had so cheerfully told along their travels. His favorite story was one about a long time player he'd never met but knew well by the name of Larry Lodish and he couldn't resist sharing it with his new team.

He told how Larry only played rather mediocre chess for an Esky-Chess alumni and how he had a horrible cold before one chess trip. Instead of canceling his plans, he went to a doctor and had his health concerns officially cleared. He didn't have a fever and outside of a severe stuffy nose and clogged sinus, there seemed no valid reason to hold him back. As long as he stayed out of the swimming pool and didn't catch a chill, chess itself certainly didn't hold any risk to making his condition any worse. The coach weighed the concerns and then gave Larry permission to go.

By some freak of chance, he managed to win his first four games of the tournament in a row. Two of the games he easily defeated lower rated players, but the other two came by means of good fortune against higher rated players that made some weird errors when they actually had him beat. The final round paired him at the number one board with the number one ranked player in the tournament. The game counted for all the first place cash and a big trophy.

Larry's illness flared worse during the final game and he couldn't control his coughing fits. The noise became so irritating that several players complained he should be kicked out of the tournament. His stomach halfway through the game grew queasy also. The men's bathroom stood about 20 paces from the tournament hall and Larry dashed into it madly and frequently. If he wasn't coughing he was gagging. The sounds he barked out were so strange that people wondered if he was killing a small horse in there. Head after head throughout the tournament hall bobbed up and smiled in amusement at his bizarre actions. Larry's opponent grew angrier and angrier as the game pressed on, while Larry continued to make great moves without hardly any thought. After he made a quick move, he'd dash back to the restroom to get some relief and not get kicked out of the tournament.

The game stayed neck and neck, winding down to a sharp endgame and it was then that Larry sneezed harder than anyone in the room had ever witnessed in their lives. Green and yellow nose drainage landed all over the board in sticky little chunks. A particularly large glob of mucus landed on his opponent's king and dangled off the top of it like a piece of living slime.

Escanaba's coach quietly handed Larry a handkerchief and had to leave the room. He held back from laughing so hard he thought his insides might break. The group of people watching the championship game started to laugh and smile at each other in disbelief. They'd never seen anything so deplorable.

Larry's opponent fumed and protested to the tournament director, but the director told him to calm down, the kid didn't do this on purpose, he felt ill. So, out of pure anger, the opponent picked up his queen and used it to tip over the grossly covered king. He gave a mean glare at Larry, shook his fist and muttered a few broken words of German at him. He then walked out of the tournament hall, never to be seen at a rated chess tournament again. With only minimal chess skill, Escanaba's sixth board Larry Lodish outlasted over 80 strong players to gain a perfect score of 5—0, win $100 first place cash and become Wisconsin's amateur champion for the year 1981.

The young Escanaba players all laughed and grinned while Jim promised the story held the honest truth. Larry had really won a tournament of a lifetime by mere good fortune. Jim told a few other interesting stories, but then switched gears and went to the topic of strategy and pep talks for the upcoming match.

"Don't let them intimidate you. Be the tougher team," Jim lectured to the kids. "This team won the league last year. If we beat them it's all downhill until they come to Esky next time. Trust me guys. We can beat this team. Remember the only thing they have on you is experience. Okay they've played in tournaments and you guys haven't. That's about to change today. Just be the tougher team."

The ride went much faster than the normal hour. Before they knew it, they were getting out of the van, grabbing their tote of chess supplies and entering Negaunee High School. Towards the cafeteria Jim led them, all the while giving them reminders and little tidbits of advice.

The nerves of the team showed and surprisingly, Jim's own nerves remained calm. Upon entering the cafeteria, they saw a small group of young men pondering a position with a heavy set coach who had dark hair and thick rimmed glasses. They looked up when they saw the Eskimos arrive and stayed in their seats not knowing what to make of a team that wore uniforms.

"Nice shirts," Negaunee's coach complimented. "We should get some of those."

The coaches shook hands and then prepared four boards for the teams to play on. Jim reached into the tote and produced four brand new chess clocks and arranged the time control for game in 30 minutes.

"Mind if we use the digital clocks?" he asked in a rhetorical manner towards Negaunee's coach.

Surprised, the big man shook his head, "not a problem at all. We should get some of those too."

After covering the rules and explaining that the match would consist of two games, the Escanaba players sat down in unison. Jim and Craig looked at each other and couldn't believe they were in such harmony. It had to be a random chance that it happened that way. Both teams waited for the go ahead and then play officially began.

The two coaches circled the boards like young hawks spying mice on a grass field. Back and forth the teams battled on and the excitement grew as Negaunee realized the Escanaba team wasn't beginners like they had earlier suspected. As the first round pushed on, Big Alan scored the first point for Escanaba with a checkmate on move eleven. The other Negaunee players looked stunned, but held fast to their games. Next Jeff punctured his opponent's defense with a fork tactic and went up a rook. Disgusted by such a devastating mistake the opponent simply resigned and Jeff didn't know what to make of it. He looked at Jim in confusion not believing a resignation came so quickly. Jim gave him a thumb's up signal letting him know the victory counted and Jeff finally relaxed.

However, Negaunee didn't give up. Their first board Owen Goodyear blitzed Greg the whole game. Greg took too much time to think and although he had a won game, he couldn't quite complete the win. A weird combination presented itself and Goodyear set a trap that Greg stumbled right into. This gave Negaunee their first point and kept them alive in the first match for a draw, only down 2-1.

The final game came down to Tyler and Negaunee's fourth board. Only a rook and a few pawns remained. Jim could tell that Negaunee's fourth board easily held enough strength to be on second board. The kid had talent and there seemed to be a nice flow to his moves. Under extreme pressure Tyler made a crucial error and gave away a free rook to a basic tactical pattern. Negaunee chalked up the second point they needed to tie the match and their coach looked like he was going to have a heart attack with excitement. At the same time Jim smiled with the thrill of the team not losing their first match. The boys had listened to him and played tough chess. He just couldn't express how proud he was of them.

"Wow, I didn't realize your Escanaba boys would play so well. Almost like old times hey Jim?" Negaunee's coach praised. "How long have these kids been playing, two years, three years?"

"Little over three months," Jim replied with a friendly grin. His pride soared. "They are a really great group of kids, I can't complain at all."

"I'm sure they are," Negaunee's coach admitted and approached his team for a quick in between match talk.

Jim took his players into the hallway and congratulated each of them for a fine, tough performance.

"You guys did it, you played tough! That was awesome, I can't believe it we drew Negaunee!"

The faces on the players were not as enthused.

"We didn't win," Greg sighed. "I lost it for the team."

"Yeah, Greg why'd you have to go and blow it," Jeff chided with some grief.

"Greg," Jim said and paused looking at his players. "Guys, come on, we played tough. This is just step one. We just hit them in the nose with a two by four. This team didn't lose a single game last year in this league, let alone draw a match. This is the best team in the U.P. and you guys just went toe to toe with them. If we keep it up, we can even beat them this next round."

"Why didn't you tell us they never lost a game last year?" Tyler asked. His disappointment of losing had carried over to his mood.

"Tyler, you have to believe that's not important. Trust me, what is important is how tough you play, not if you win or lose. If you play tough chess, winning will certainly follow. We have another game and in scholastic chess, you might just turn the tables and win the next round. Anything can happen. Focus on being tough, not on winning. I'm telling you guys the wins will happen all by themselves just play tough. Now, hands in."

They all made a fist with their hands and put them together in a circle.

"Play tough," Jim announced and they all bumped their fists together. "Esky-chess Express, here we come for round two."

Both teams sat down and rotated the boards for a color change. The coaches instructed them to begin and they all fought right out of the gates like tigers. Negaunee's coach had made a few adjustments, and his players seemed to start off with better positions. They also had more fight in their eyes and were set to prove that the last round was a fluke. To them, Escanaba would take their proper place of being the second best team.

The excitement became too much for Jim and his nerves started to flair up. He took a seat where his team could see him, but he just meditated. He could hear move after move being completed and when he looked up he saw Greg with a frown.

"Same thing, he blitzed me again. I had him beat and I lost on time."

"It's okay Greg, you played tough. I know what to do to fix that. Trust me next time you play him, you'll win both games. You're much better than he is, we'll get him next time."

Greg smiled and went over to the boards to support his team. The games raged on and it was Jeff who came over with a sad frown on his face. Dejected Jim felt ready to give him a solid handshake and wish him well, but the young man's nose lifted and his teeth burst into a huge smile.

"Psyche," Jeff exclaimed, "took him down."

Jeff's win tied up the match. Jim couldn't resist looking on as everyone else watched the final two games wind down. Tyler and his opponent came to a near identical position as the last game. This time, Tyler put more care and set a trap for his opponent. Like a rabbit getting a leg snagged up in a snare, Tyler's opponent had to give up a rook or lose. In desperation, he tried to conjure a life saving defense, but Tyler would not be denied his revenge. He snapped back with a fast checkmate and the Eskimos held a 2-1 lead.

Big Alan's game left the fate of the match in the balance. He was up a full bishop for free and the Esky players just wished it to be over soon. However, the

Negaunee player had much experience in the endgame and won the bishop back. This evened the game as time ran down to only a couple minutes for each player.

Move after move they parried each other's threats and tried to break the other's defenses. On Big Alan's next turn, he made a strange king move and Jim instantly calculated a loss. The move definitely was an error, but not an obvious one. It seemed at the same moment Big Alan saw the loss too, but before his opponent could make a move, he offered him a verbal draw. By this time everyone else watching saw the winning move for the Negaunee player. Surely he would decline the offer, win the game and tie up the second match. Instead he foolishly grasped Big Alan's hand and accepted the draw! Escanaba had snatched a surprise victory and won the second match by the score of 2.5—1.5.

The Negaunee player's hearts sank in disbelief and proceeded to razz their comrade for his outrageous mistake. Negaunee's coach then proceeded to give both teams a winded speech on how one should never take a draw without checking the score of the match first. The Negaunee team looked downcast about the loss that shouldn't have been, but they took it with grace and good sportsmanship. Negaunee's coach walked over to Jim and congratulated him.

"Good job Jim, you've done a wonderful job with these kids."

Jim shook inside with delight. "Thanks. Sorry to take the win in this manner, we were fortunate. The match itself though was very well played by both teams."

"We haven't had that kind of excitement in a long time, hopefully the other teams aren't as strong as you guys were today," Negaunee's coach replied.

The players talked a little chess and shared a couple different opening moves they knew with each other. The two teams had a mutual liking for each other and after a peaceful goodbye and a pleasant challenge for the next time they met, the Escanaba team got into their van and headed for supper.

"Tradition guys, if we win, we go to Burger World," Jim stated.

"Yes, I love Burger World," Jeff shouted.

"It's an old Escanaba tradition to go to Burger World whenever we win a match, tournament or someone plays outstanding. You guys played tough chess today, it was outstanding."

"I lost both my games," Greg muttered. "But I had fun too. Thanks for saving the day guys."

"Greg you played tough. Everyone played tough," Jim praised. "We won too. I told you guys, be tough and the winning follows all by itself."

"Except for Craig, he didn't play," Big Alan joked out loud.

Everyone laughed and gave Craig a friendly punch in the arm.

"Oh guys, with winning comes a treat."

"What treat?" they inquired.

"A cherry slush with vanilla ice cream. That is our team treat for winning."

Several of the players shouted for joy about the victory and for support of the reward process. Craig sat back in his seat and appeared a little dismayed.

"What's wrong Craig," Jim asked and looked at him in the rearview mirror.

"I would rather get the slush with cola flavor instead, not cherry flavor."

The van went silent, almost as if he had insulted a Catholic priest. Jeff started to pound his fist into the palm of his other hand and forced a huge frown.

"I wouldn't do that," Big Alan countered with a huge frown of his own.

"Well on second thought, cherry is my second favorite flavor out of two flavors to choose from. Let's go with cherry."

Jim gave a big smile. "You guys, let's make a deal with Craig. If we win States, we'll think about letting him have a cola slush instead of cherry one, does that sound all right?"

The team laughed as they pulled up to the restaurant and went inside to eat. They had won their first ever chess match and Jim couldn't believe the excitement in their eyes. At that moment coaching chess had been the best thing that ever happened to him.

CHAPTER 9

▼

A WEAK LINK

Things continued in an unbelievable positive direction for the chess team. Win after win they chalked up against the Upper Peninsula teams. They worked extremely hard at continuing to improve and didn't lose a single match the rest of the season. Even when Negaunee came to Escanaba for the return match, they didn't stand a chance against the fiery and now somewhat experienced Eskimos. The Eskimos defeated Negaunee 4—0 both times and earned a right to try for a state championship title.

The local newspaper also started printing small articles on behalf of their success. The media generally felt chess to be a simple hobby and paid it little attention. However, when the Eskimos started to dominate the league a spark of interest generated and the paper covered their scores and tournament results. This gave the fledgling team a big boost of confidence.

The magic of the team appeared perfect on the outside. On the inside it appeared to be a different story. Jeff although playing some of the best chess on the team constantly seemed to be depressed or irritable. Jim could sense Jeff's desire to be on first board, but he also noticed the frustration of it not happening. Greg too had realized Jeff started to chase his top spot after the early losses to Goodyear and decided to double time it himself on practice in order to fend off the challenge. Both players won all their games the rest of the season and tension started to flare up between them.

Even though they both benefited from the struggle and gained incredible chess strength, the competition for the top job eased out of hand. Both were certainly strong enough to lead the team, but only one player could be on first board. Jim thought long and hard over it and decided that Greg held the tiniest of leadership edges and although a tough decision, he decided to keep Greg on first board and Jeff at second.

Other players on the team were affected by it also and dropped hints to Jim on how they felt. Jim's nerves flared each time he'd listen to their informative comments. The team was so close to being perfect and after all they kept winning. He just couldn't bring himself to tamper with a formula that won. Still, he wondered why one little defect seemed to be dragging the whole system down and wouldn't just go away.

He wanted to talk to Ole Cookie, but Ole Cookie was covering his shift and although not living up totally to the assistant coaching position like initially discussed, he still aided Jim in a valuable manner by covering and swapping shifts at work to make chess possible. His mind nagged him to not sit idle on the matter and that the problem should be addressed in some fashion to keep the team from going backwards. He didn't know if he should talk to Jeff alone, or talk to the whole team. Losing Jeff scared him to death and he didn't want to reproach the young fellow too severely for fear he might quit. Such a move could have their championship run fizzle before it even started.

Finally he decided to work up enough courage and talk to Jeff by himself and be real passive on the communication. He had worked with Greg enough to know he could handle the stress responsibly and again the problem appeared not to be too serious. He asked Jeff to stay after club one night and they talked together about winning States.

The conversation went smooth, but Jim read Jeff's face and it told him he did not feel he was the second best chess player on the team. Jeff's eyes gave the message he deserved to be playing on first board and although the young man appeared peaceful in his words, an emotion of jealousy radiated from his presence.

Jim remained calm, explained the situation and tried to get Jeff to focus on the tournament portion of States instead. He told how they were a team and that he needed to be concerned about winning five games period, not whether those wins came on board one or two. He explained that the consolation was they did have individual awards for board performances, so a great individual performance would still be rewarded even if a team itself didn't do well and that there was no need to worry about honors. However at that moment Jim pictured himself throwing his own trophy from States in the garbage can and felt inside that maybe this choice example wasn't the best. Jeff on the other hand liked the incentives of personal reward and relaxed a bit.

Jim also explained how he had never been first board on his own teams and that it didn't matter, just being a tough player was all that was asked. Jeff calmed some more, but he did clash at Jim's logic with a quip about the infamous lapse of 1989 that cost the championship. The whole idea of losing a won title appeared to make Jeff ill and he couldn't seem to compute nor forgive such a horrendous error.

Jim sat back and realized Jeff's emotions. The kid acted in a positive manner at least, but he didn't feel right with the message and continued to remain calm even though his hands shook in his lap.

Jeff in terms of skill would certainly lose ten out of ten in a heartbeat if he and Jim ever played that many serious games. Yet, he just couldn't give the coach the proper respect he deserved because it ate him inside that Jim showed this crazy weakness of not finishing off an opponent when it counted. It just didn't make sense to him and it bothered him deeply and he refused to discuss it with his coach and didn't want to be associated at all with the weakness part of Jim. Instead, he wanted to show people and the team he could do better and this he could only prove by playing in the top spot of the team. So he too remained calm and silent.

The talk did have its benefit and Jeff although bluffing did follow the proper channel and was polite. States was a go and the chess team showed all signs of being in tact. Jim still had a few weeks to bring things together for a wonderful drive at the title and even though a piece of the team still seemed to be missing, they would take a shot at the title.

*   *   *   *

Sitting at his board, Jim studied a deep position from a game between future opponents from other teams. A brisk knock at the door took him by surprise. As he approached to answer he saw the handle jiggle, turn a couple times and then the door opened wide. With a gust of cold air came a huge surprise. Walters turned the corner of the door holding a large suitcase, while a taxicab spun away in the background.

"What the heck are you doing home?" he asked with revelation, shaking Walter's hand with a firm grip. "You're not due back until April."

"Sorry I didn't get a chance to tell you. It was either grab this vacation and flight on 15 minutes notice or wait until the snow melted," Walters smiled. "This is better anyway, I've got two weeks off and I can help you guys train for States."

"Oh is it ever great to see you!"

The two made some tea in the kitchen and Jim told how in three weeks they'd be traveling down to Detroit for the championships. He mentioned how nervous he was, but didn't say anything about the Jeff problem. Rather he played it cool and positive and looked forward to Walter's technical help in preparation for the big tournament.

"I'll play all your players this week," Walters said. "Tuesday and Friday, and then next week I can work one on one with each of them. We'll get them ready," he pounded his fist on the coffee table, proud to be part of the action. "What do you have for time off?"

"I have to serve a banquet dinner on Saturday, work regular cafeteria on Sunday and then I could take a 10 day vacation if I wanted. You want me to?"

"Yeah I want you to, I want to get some hard core chess in and I wouldn't mind doing a little ice fishing."

"Oh the walleyes are biting on the bay too, the season ends soon. I have our shack out there right now. Want to go tonight?"

"You know, I wanted to play you some chess, but yeah, I'm dying to go fishing. Let's go."

Jim grabbed the gear and although Walters was vastly underdressed for winter from being stationed in the Middle East for so long he bundled the best he could and stood ready to trek through the deep frozen snow that covered the lake. It didn't take them long to get to the wooden shanty and go inside. Jim lit a fire in the wood stove and grabbed a metal ice scoop. Their holes had a layer of ice over them only an inch or so thick. With the back of the tool he jabbed the ice until it broke and then scooped the floating ice chunks to the side. They put bait on their hooks and their lines in the water. The two relaxed under the light of a propane lantern and watched their bobbers float in the little hole of water. They caught up on how their lives were going and every now and then a bobber sunk under the water hushing them both immediately. When the bobber went far enough under, whoever had the bite gave the line a jerk and pulled up a fish through the hole.

The following week Walters took the team on in a series of challenges and as predicted he crushed each and every one of them with the exception of Jeff. Jeff's style matched well against Walters. The young man cleverly planned to hit aggression with aggression and normally this worked well against his big opponent. However, Walters having far more experience knew to switch the game to a more passive stance and ground Jeff down. The game remained close the whole way and Walters ended up squeezing a difficult victory in a king and pawn endgame only because he had one extra move. Walters congratulated the young man on a fine performance and tried to complement him further, but Jeff had left the room already in frustration.

"What's up with him?" Walters asked and the rest of the room went silent.

"He gets quite emotional, it's nothing to worry over," Jim replied.

"Yeah, he really hates to lose," Tyler added.

Walters continued the next week with an endgame lecture that Jim had kicked himself for not thinking of showing himself. The kids loved Walter's help and he measured and weighed them all and trained them the best he knew how for such short timing before States. This gave Jim a breather to concentrate on other chess matters and he prepared the team's travel schedule, parent permission forms and membership matters for pre-registration.

With the exception of a quick trip to Walter's mother's house, night after night the two either played chess or went fishing. On one cold evening they decided to drink tea and play blitz chess all night long. Without much effort Jim got the best of his friend nearly every game. About every ten games Walters would gain a rare draw and once in awhile he came up with some trick that made Jim think and lose by using too much time.

"Gosh I can't believe how strong you've gotten at chess," Walters replied tipping his king over yet again.

"Maybe it's time for me to start teaching you how to play instead of you teaching me?" Jim grinned. "Do you want some more abuse?"

"Nah, I give. You're just too strong, for now. I'll have to do some homework and try again the next visit."

"When are you coming back again do you think?" Jim asked.

"I don't know, might be a year, maybe a year and a half. I extended my tour of the Persian Gulf," Walters paused and looked a little apologetic. "Sometimes it's the only way to promote and get ahead in the system. It's going to be tough, I drive one ship home shortly and then take command of a brand new one heading right back."

Jim shrugged and showed he was clearly not comfortable with how long his friend had scheduled to be gone.

"I met a girl on the ship."

"You did?" Jim tapped his friend on the arm. "Why didn't you tell me earlier?"

"Well, we shouldn't, but we sneak around a little bit on the ship. With the 21st century rules and all, I can't let on to anyone that I'm seeing someone under my administration, or I can get grieved for favoritism and all that jolly stuff. It's really not worth the risk, but you know me I can't resist the company of a fine woman."

"Ouch, that doesn't sound good for a relationship."

"No it isn't, but at least we both understand how the system works. I'm sure the little fling won't last. She loves me, but I'm hesitant. I've never been one to commit long term to a woman. I just can't see getting stuck on the old proverbial ball and chain. I like my freedom. How about you, you seeing anybody?"

"No," Jim coughed. "Not really. I wish. I have a nice car and all, but in the winter it runs horrible in the snow. It's the last thing girls want."

"Come on, seriously."

"No, really. Between work and the team, I just don't get to meet women. The time will come soon enough I'm sure."

Walters refilled their teas with hot water and came back to the living room, while Jim sat on the sofa and clicked a movie on the large screen television.

"Besides, I'd have to share this big television you bought," Jim said and laughed.

Walters laughed also and relaxed. "You've done a wonderful job with that chess team. I can't believe how good they are."

Jim tensed up a little bit, he could sense Walters wanted to talk to him about something important regarding the team and he wasn't sure what.

"I try my best," Jim replied. "I'm concerned because we've never lost a match yet though, we both know that can't last forever."

"I agree," Walters shrugged. "I'm not sure you can win States this year. Maybe second tops, most likely third or fourth."

"Why not?" Jim asked as his stomach fell to the floor. Walters seemed to be right ninety-nine percent of the time about anything he ever had an opinion on, this little prediction threw him for a loop. Jim knew a moment of truth had come. "We will field the toughest team. You know that?"

"Toughest doesn't always win when the chemistry isn't right. I hate to say it, but the way I see it, you only have three-fourths of a team. Please don't take it personal."

Jim sat on the sofa and stayed quiet. He now could see clear as daylight the problem of his team. That one little defect of not cooperating 100 percent had bad potential. This worked for them at first because they grew strong in competition, now it might have possibly cost them the state championship before they even tried.

"It's like our team in 1989, someone will mess it up," Walters continued. He then put his hand up, "I'm not talking about your game. We only had three-fourths of a team also, but it was because of Rodriguez and his crazy attitude and style. Losing States really wasn't your fault. It wasn't anybody's fault. We just didn't have the right chemistry. I've studied this team of yours Jim and they don't have it right now."

Jim's heart now sank with his stomach. "Are we doomed to lose?"

"Not necessarily," Walters paused and took a sip of tea, "but you have got to pull that Jeff kid online with the rest of them somehow. They get along like they've been life long friends, barring Jeff. He's an outsider and although the other kids don't hate him, he is rather offensive."

"He's a good kid, he just has social problems."

"Rodriguez was a good person too, and is successful in life. I'd buy the guy a beer tomorrow and sit down and chat with him in a minute. But, that doesn't mean I'd want him on my chess team again."

"The kid is a strong player you saw him, he went toe to toe with you."

"You're a strong player too and you of all people know there is an intangible to winning that isn't apparent in chess strength," Walters stopped and realized he had said enough negative things. "I'm not trying to jinx you, I really apologize for that. I just want you to not get your hopes up this year. It's the first year. You have three years with this group. The good news is I feel ultimately confident that within one of those years, you have a legitimate crack at winning a state championship, maybe even with only three-fourths of a team."

"We want it this year."

"It's a good spirit to have, please prove me wrong," Walters reasoned, while Jim sipped his tea.

They stayed quiet for a while and although Jim wanted to become angry with his friend he didn't have it in him. Walters meant the world to him and after all, maybe he was right, he was right most of the time on anything else. Walters also felt like he may have said too many negative words and wanted to repair the mood a little bit.

"You're a great chess coach," Walters commented, slightly fixing his friend's confidence. "Much greater than I ever thought. Perhaps I'm wrong and you can corral those young guys into winning this thing. And if anyone can make the intangibles work it's you buddy. The chess gods certainly owe you one. You'll do it. You'll find a way. Just stick with your theme of being the toughest team. With a tough chess team, we both know that anything can happen," Walters finished bringing back a peaceful moment.

Heavy white snow fell outside while the two chatted the rest of the evening about different things. In the morning Jim drove Walters to the airport. His Mustang slid all over the ice, but they made it safely. They gave each other a firm handshake and Walters got into the plane. Jim waved goodbye and watched the airplane takeoff. He wanted to go home, but felt compelled to stay and watch the plane disappear into the sky. A cold chill ran down his spine and he wasn't sure if it was his nerves from a bad premonition or the freezing lashes of the ten below zero wind biting at his face. Either way only a few days remained before he took the team to Detroit to play in the biggest tournament of his player's lives.

CHAPTER 10

▼

THE FUN OF A CHESS TRIP

The morning of the departure for States had finally arrived. The team met early Friday morning and packed the school van. Because Detroit was so far away from Escanaba, they had permission to leave school a day early and they took advantage of the situation. The newness of the moment kept the team excited and they all entered the van with a sense of pride. Even Jeff had a smile on his face. He went back to the farthest seat in the van and sat alone with his sunglasses on and his arms crossed, all the while enjoying the moment of importance.

Before they pulled out of the school driveway, Jim double-checked to make sure they all had their uniform shirts. He spent most of the previous evening admiring his own coach's shirt and didn't want anyone to forget how important this was. Some teams from downstate would have their own chess shirts and of course Flint would be wearing theirs so the Eskimos needed to follow suit. Although overly repeating himself, Jim continued to tell them that the shirts made the team look organized and strong. This was an advantage they could ill afford to give away for free.

The van began the long journey and nobody displayed any interest in eating breakfast. Some players had pre-tournament jitters extinguish their hunger, while others just flat out refused to consider morning as a time to feed. Understanding this Jim announced that the van had a full tank of gas to start with and that when they reached the halfway point in Gaylord, they would stop and eat at a customary Mexican restaurant that Esky players from the past always visited on the way down to States.

The magnetic board soon circled the middle seat for one game of chess after another. Greg sat in the front passenger seat, as was tradition for first board to do so by previous teams. He and Jim chatted along the way, the three players in the middle played chess the whole ride, while Jeff; still serene in the moment simply enjoyed the ride.

The travel time went by fast. Before Jim knew it he ushered the players to a table in the restaurant. They wasted no time and dipped colored nacho chips into a variety of salsas, some hot while others mild. They all joked and a couple players ended up daring Big Alan with a dollar each, to see if he'd eat a whole hot pepper. The dare was foolish, because Big Alan was conditioned to the food and ate the pepper like most regular people could eat a carrot.

The regular meals finally arrived and they carried on enjoying their lunch. The most entertaining moment happened when a noodle from Tyler's soup slid off his plate and gravity gave it a playful life of its own. The group watched in amazement as it wobbled off the table to the floor. Craig's eyes opened wide and he turned and dug into his backpack that he carried with him. Producing his biology book, he flipped madly through the pages and found his spot. Opening the book wide, he pointed to a picture and showed it to the group.

"My goodness that thing looks exactly like the virus here on page 74," he exclaimed in a proud voice.

Everyone laughed, mostly with clean humor at Craig, not with him. However, the noodle did appear to be a realistic oversized model of a virus as he claimed.

"If only you were as observant in protecting your queen as you are with taking care of that biology book! You'd be a crusher," Tyler joked, tapping his friend in the arm while the group all laughed with good nature.

After lunch, because he held the lowest position on the team, Craig had the mandatory duty of filling the vehicle up with gas. This he did like a pro without complaint and the team continued to travel. The trip took almost 10 hours total of driving and by the time they had arrived at the hotel their tummies yearned for more food. They decided to go to a local mall that had a large food court with a variety of store window restaurants to choose from. Everyone seemed to decide on eating different types of food that ranged from fried rice to steak sandwiches and cheddar fries. For a drink though, Jim couldn't help but pass the passion he and Walters enjoyed on their own so much in the past, the infamous strawberry smoothie.

"My goodness, we must make getting a smoothie part of our future pre-tournament traditions," Jim announced and the idea was well received. A couple players joined him in buying another.

The trip down had been as peaceful as Jim could have asked for even though his own nerves had started to bobble in uncomfortable twitches. The team made it to Detroit safe, they were well fed and the players showed no animosity. That was the way the first day of a chess trip was supposed to be, nothing but fun and travel. They shopped around the mall for an hour and then returned to the hotel to swim in the pool. One of the players had bought a small foam football and they tossed it around until the skin on their hands and feet became wrinkled. They capped the night off by getting a couple chess boards out and watching television while they practiced what they could for the last time. At 11:00 PM, Jim ordered lights out and went to his room in the adjoining suite.

The players joked and giggled to calm their anxiety and then eventually succumbed to sleep. Jim on the other hand, tossed and turned all night. He did feel some relief in that at least he didn't have to perform, so he could get by easily without proper sleep. Too much was on the line for his mind to relax, Saturday and Sunday would be their biggest chess experience ever as a team.

✳   ✳   ✳   ✳

Early Saturday morning, a light snow fell outside the hotel and covered the sidewalk with a light coat. Jim felt glad not to see the huge piles of the stuff like they had back home. Relief took his mind away from driving. Going to a restaurant for breakfast and then to the tournament site to play would be smooth today. He woke the team up and although quite groggy they moved like sloth out of their beds. They changed into their uniform shirts and in no time had some spirit. Like the previous morning they didn't have much interest in eating, but this time Jim had a different approach.

"You guys don't realize this, but you have got to eat and have energy for your long day," he lectured and didn't even realize it. The players perked up and looked at him in a calm tone. "Trust me, when we get back here at about midnight tonight, you are going to be more tired than you've ever been at anything before. I'm telling you, this will be as exhausting as any physical sport you could ever partake in."

"You're kidding right?" Big Alan asked. "I was willing to eat breakfast anyway."

Jim smiled and realized he needed to calm down, his insides rattled like a jack-hammer. "Well, I don't mean it as serious as I guess I said it. But no, I'm not kidding, you guys will feel a type of exhaustion tonight like you've never felt before, a type of emotional exhaustion I can't explain or describe. All I can say is, that in about 14 or 15 hours, you'll see what I mean," he smiled and led his team to the van.

The team packed their personal gear. Craig had yet another mandatory duty at this point and that was to carry the chess tote back and forth and to make sure the starters had good access and availability to any equipment, pens or score-sheets they might need. After loading it into the van, they stopped at a greasy spoon and ate breakfast. After filling themselves completely, they next made a quick stop at a gas station and Jim instructed them to load up on refreshments and snacks and to put them in the tote or their backpacks in case playing went so long they didn't get a chance to leave for lunch or supper.

"No lunch or supper?" Tyler asked. "Is that possible?"

"It sure could happen I'm afraid, has happened to me many times. That's why we need snacks on the side, so we have some fuel if we need it," Jim instructed.

Again they piled into the van and searched for the tournament sight. Jim was horrible at driving in areas he had never been to before. However, he planned wisely and printed off a map at home from the internet ahead of time. After some prompt navigation from Greg they arrived at a high school nestled deep in an urban neighborhood.

"All right guys, you remember the rules," Jim announced. "No leaving the school without talking to me first. Is this clear?"

"Yes dad," Tyler kidded.

"And no going anywhere alone, we must be in groups of two or greater we know," Greg followed.

"And win all your games too!" Jeff added and the rest of the team lifted their eyebrows in surprise laughter to actually hear Jeff crack a joke.

"Not just win," Jim replied, but in a motivated voice. "Be the toughest team. Remember, we're going to be the toughest team here this weekend. They don't know who we are today, but they will know who we are Sunday evening at the trophy presentation."

"Yeah," the team exclaimed together. They could feel the energy in their bones.

They walked into the school where they followed signs that led them to a cafeteria that had lunch tables set for registration and waiting. The actual playing room was off to the side and the doors to it were shut tight as nobody was allowed to wander around. About the cafeteria the Eskimos went unnoticed. They just appeared to be another hack team that would get pummeled by the big schools.

Jim told how the wait would be one of the longest and most impatient in their lives, but that they should just relax and keep calm. His own nerves tumbled inside him. He walked up to the tournament director and introduced himself and then finalized his registration papers by listing his starters. They were now fully taken care of until round one began, less than an hour away.

Back and forth the team paced and they appeared like they might suffer from old age before they ever got a chance to play any chess. They thought about getting some boards out, but there was too much fretfulness to think about chess until the tournament started. Question after question they bounced off Jim and their simple mindset started to border on ridiculous. All they had to do was simply wait and see. For the first time in his coaching career he became a little impatient.

"I'm sorry guys, but sheesh, why didn't you ask me these questions sooner?" he realized he was barking from his own nervousness and impatience and rounded up his team for better instructional talk. "Guys," he put his hands up to mean peace, "we're going to be okay, remember the toughest team can overcome anything. Play tough, that's all you need to worry about doing." He focused them with his words and they responded fully by first quieting down and then showing their game faces that they meant business. They just watched other teams as the room filled almost to capacity. Consumed they felt like a drop of water in a lake, but they kept their mindset on playing their first opponents.

Soon the tournament director gave an announcement, and covered certain topics regarding time controls, prizes, and tie-breaks. When he was finished he posted the pairings and instructed the teams to find their proper tables and prepare to begin playing. A wave of players and coaches descended on the charts and movement was difficult because of the congestion.

Jim noticed right away that his team was ranked at the bottom out of 32 teams. Dead last because none of his players were rated except for Greg. The Eskimos were paired against Birch Run on table 16, a team Jim had read about but didn't know well. He led his players into the tournament room, showed them their table and noted how the system was just like back home, only a bit larger of a room. The players sat in unison and waited for the other team to show up. They were ready to play chess.

CHAPTER 11

▼

STATES

The Birch Run players showed up to the table one at a time and sat across from the Eskimos, while Jim stood quietly off to the side of the room. He noted how Birch Run's team all wore long trench coats, shabby T-shirts and tattered jeans. All but one of their players had long hair, yet they appeared to be a good-natured group of kids. A great chess team they probably were not Jim figured and at the same time he wished dearly that his team would not be flat for the first round.

Birch Run's coach entered the room and was a stark contrast to his team's image. He looked more like a gym teacher than a chess instructor. Although not very tall, he had a sturdy build and wore a shiny gold watch along with a sharp gold ring on his right hand. His glasses matched his outfit as the frames displayed a high-class pattern of gold. Recognizing the matching shirt of the opposing team, he wandered over to Jim holding his cup of coffee and introduced himself. The two shook hands and Jim's cold and clammy palm gave away his emotional status.

"First year coaching?" the Birch Run coach asked with a scratchy voice. Jim nodded. "Where you guys from, I don't think I've seen that name before, Escanaba?"

"The Upper Peninsula," Jim replied a bit fearful. He tried to remember if he recognized this guy from 1989 at all, but the man's face appeared new to him.

The tournament director had instructed for play to begin and the familiar lunge of chess clocks echoed across the room.

"You got a big school up there?"

"Not really, Escanaba only has about a population of 12,000 give or take."

"Wow," Birch Run's coach said in surprise, "that is tiny."

The opposing coach appeared quite calm. He didn't even seem one bit worried about his team's chances, good or bad.

"How long have you been coaching this Birch Run group?"

"Oh, about five years now. This is the best group I've actually ever had. Great bunch they are, although I'm fearful of drugs in a couple of them when they get to college."

Jim couldn't imagine coaching for five years, everything with his team was so new and exciting in every way that only the present consumed him, not the past or future. He looked across the room at the 120 plus high school students and how every now and then a game finished and the players got up to record their results with their coach and the tournament director. The whole scene had a kind of majestic beauty to it, until he looked up at the top board and saw Dillard Senior and the rest of the Flint squad.

"That Dillard kid is the highest rated player in the state for his age," the Birch Run coach exclaimed after noticing Jim was looking at them. "Their coach won the Michigan Open last year. They're tough."

Jim felt shy. The coach didn't know that Dillard Senior won only on tie-breaks, against him and Walters no less. Still, Jim decided to try and get some information from his newfound friend.

"What do you know about those Dillards?"

"Not a lot, just that we seemed to get paired against them every single year and they just give us a scha-lacking. I don't know what I have to do to get my kids past them. They're like professionals," he finished sipping his coffee and his interest seemed to drop immediately. "Well, I'm going to blend in for awhile, nice meeting you and good luck with your Escanaba team."

"Good luck to you too," Jim replied. At that moment he saw Jeff execute a checkmate on second board. "You're going to need it," he whispered under his breath to himself feeling calm and collected now.

Greg soon brought the team another checkmate and Big Alan went up two rooks. The toughest game of the match loomed on fourth board where Tyler fought for his king's life. He had made a tactical error around move 15 and had been paying dearly for it. His position had been compromised most of the game, but under Jim's strict guidance to never resign he battled on as if the game were level. Slowly he wore the game down to an even position and then through a gross blunder by the Birch Run player, he completed the first round 4-0 sweep for the Eskimos.

"Ah, Mr. B was right," Tyler told the other players, folding up his score-sheet. "I was cooked like a goose that whole game and look, I won that. Don't ever resign!"

The team ate lunch and then headed back to the tournament for round two. They were paired against Clio this time on Table 8 and in unison that is where they went. Jim realized that after chatting so much with Birch Run's coach, he forgot to keep statistics on the match. Craig looked bored to him and a numbers assignment seemed to fit him perfectly. After getting out a blank tablet of paper and a pen, he instructed Craig for every round this time forward to jot down the opposing team, its player's names, their ratings and most importantly the results of each game. Craig gave a large grin to show the task selected had been a good one for him and he set to work on it, adding some extra details along the way.

With one less thing to worry about, Jim relaxed, but again he looked up at Table 1, where Terry Dillard seemed to be having a field day with his opponent. Dillard Senior watched every move his team made and paced back and forth like he was in harmony with a clock's pendulum. Jim no sooner glanced at his team and Jeff was getting up from his board with a big smile on his face. He gave Jim a thumb's up signal to show he had won his game in a super fast fashion. The rest of the Eskimos looked on and took a charge from this.

Clio had considerable more talent that Birch Run did, but again the Eskimos ground them down. Greg finished with a brilliant checkmate, while Big Alan drew and Tyler won giving the team a 3.5—.5 victory and still enough time remained to go get supper before the next round.

The team piled into the van and decided spaghetti was best for supper. It had a lot of carbohydrates, would process easy and they all liked it. The team didn't joke around. Rather they continued to keep their game-faces on. They were serious and at the same time seemed to be having the time of their lives. Jim couldn't believe they pushed through the first two teams with such ease. The team remained in good spirits. Jeff showed no sign of problem and even his anxiety seemed to be focused on playing good chess. The day went as planned up to this point.

On the way back, Jim kept up with his toughest team approach and never 'resign' philosophy. The players took this advice with more seriousness than ever. They were going to start playing the big boys now and they needed to continue to give it their absolute best efforts.

When they arrived back at the tournament, they noticed they were paired against Monroe High School at Table 4. Monroe was already there and waiting for the Eskimos. They donned their green and white chess shirts and Jim could feel the impact of such a strong psychological tactic used against him now. The Esky players took their place and headed into battle. The tournament director started the round and the sound of chess clocks rushed through the room. Jim paced behind his team and almost bumped into Dillard Senior doing the same thing. Dillard Senior looked up in astonishment and then relaxed.

"Hi Jim," he whispered his greeting, but offered no handshake. "Are you here to see us win another state championship?"

"I hope not," Jim replied and walked away. He wanted to worry about the Eskimos, not Flint. However, he had this sixth sense that Dillard Senior would pay more attention to his players now that they were on the top tables. Nobody seemed to be putting a dent in the Flint team as they held the number one table with relative ease up to this point.

Two hours went by in the round. Flint had their opponents pretty well taken care of while all four of the Escanaba games were even. Jim hoped his players had the stamina to make it through this grueling third round. The players had played lots of chess so far today and he could see a yawn every now and then that made him cringe.

Jeff came through and sparked the team again when his opponent dropped a pawn in the endgame. It still took Jeff 25 more moves to win, but they were easy moves spent checking to make sure he didn't blunder his win away. With his victory in hand, he gave the rest of the team strength. Monroe's first board was a strong junior player and although Greg threw everything he could at the young man, the game ended in a rook and bishop versus rook and bishop textbook draw. Tyler couldn't hang onto his game and erred on some calculation and lost a nail-biter.

Big Alan's game was the last game going in the tournament room. The time was nearing midnight and the game didn't look to be ending any time soon. The Flint players watched for a while after they won their match to see if this unknown Escanaba team was for real or not, but even they fatigued and went back to their hotel. Move after move Big Alan fought to keep his team alive. The rest of the Eskimos just sat and waited in a mindset of fog and even some doubt.

Jim tried to sit down and then got right back up and watched the game. He examined the position again and again, it was dead even. A draw kept them undefeated, but they'd lose half a point in the standings, something they could ill afford against a powerhouse team like Flint. A win however, kept them tied for first place and their chances for a state title alive.

Big Alan sat and stared at the board for a long time. Jim saw a move he should make, but fought off a yawn himself. He couldn't figure out what his player could be thinking about. Finally, Big Alan made his move, wrote it down and hit his clock with authority. This startled Jim, the Monroe player and the other Esky players that waited. Nobody seemed to know what was going on or what Big Alan planned in his mind.

Jim looked at his move and frowned, it could only be a lemon. However, Big Alan smiled like he had the game easily won and Jim couldn't figure this out. Finally, Jim pulled up a chess set in his mind and started some hard-core calculation and it was only then he could see what Big Alan was up to. Sure enough, although one barely visible error led to another, there was a zugzwang for his poor opponent in 11 moves exactly. The series was brilliant and along the lines of strong master play.

Jim looked at Big Alan and lit up with a smile. Although they hadn't spoken a word, they had communicated. Big Alan would win this game and Jim went to reassure the other teammates they had a great chance to remain undefeated. 15 minutes later, the Monroe player resigned and Escanaba entered into a four-way tie for first place.

Jim and Craig gathered up all the chess gear and everyone loaded into the van for the trip back to the hotel.

"You were right Mr. B, I'm more tired than I've ever been in my life," whined Tyler.

"Yeah," Greg said. "How did you know that? I feel like I've been crushed by a rock."

"Yaawwwh," Big Alan tried to say but fell asleep before the van stopped.

"Craig, are you tired?" Jim asked with a smirk.

"Hardly, you were right though, look at these guys they're drained."

"Yeah, I am emotionally spent. I can't believe it took that much out of me," Jeff added.

The team straggled back to their hotel room and went to bed immediately. Only Craig brushed his teeth and when he got into his sleeping bag, the rest of the players had already fallen asleep. Jim went to his suite and collapsed on his bed. Even though he didn't play, he had the same exhaustion as the players; a combination of fatigue, stress and nerves all bundled into one. He actually didn't mind. After day one his Eskimos showed the mettle to be the toughest team in the room. The possibility existed that Walters might be wrong about them and before he fell asleep he thought maybe they did have the right chemistry after all to win this thing. The Eskychess Express ran its engines with power this day.

*   *   *   *

The phone rang early in the morning and Jim answered it. The operator stated that this was his wake-up call and Jim thanked her for her courtesy and proceeded to wake up the boys. He half expected the task of getting the team up to be near impossible. To his surprise all it took was one word and they wrestled up like soldiers in boot camp and dressed.

All their signs of fatigue from the previous night had vanished. Food is what they craved now and they soon found themselves in the van driving to an I.H.O.P. for breakfast. Jim had a hunger for pancakes along with sausage, bacon, eggs and a cool glass of milk.

They ate their food in silence at the restaurant and filled themselves with energy. Jim ate pancake after pancake like he'd never tasted them in his life before. Still his nerves rattled with excitement. They all sat in a serious manner and counted the minutes until they played the next round.

They paid their bill and left a tip and then headed to the tournament site. Jim wanted to lecture them, but they remained silent, focused and he decided to be quiet for a change. Nothing would help them now. Their mood was perfect for a championship run. All their hard work came down to a chance to win it now.

When they arrived at the tournament they noticed other teams looking at them. They wanted to know who this Escanaba team was that started the tournament ranked last and now sat on second board playing the highly visible number two ranked team: Detroit Dayton. Dayton a private school for serious scholars only, wore solid red chess shirts and their players were easily seen throughout the room. The Esky players found their spot, while Jim watched the Flint team assemble into their position on Table 1. The Eskimos bumped fists together for good luck and the tournament director gave the go ahead to begin.

Dillard Senior now started to scout Escanaba and made notes on a laptop computer he carried. Jim wanted to keep notes on what was happening, but he couldn't bring himself to mess with the focus of his team. For some reason he felt inside that it would be an Escanaba vs. Flint showdown for the state title. He kind of grunted under his breath and wondered why it couldn't have been any other team except them. His players though appeared to be up for the challenge and this helped. If Flint wanted a real chess match, the Eskimos would give them everything they ever asked for in an opponent. Today was the day.

Round four drew on and it was Tyler who struck gold first. He had managed to tie up his opponent in knots and strangled the poor guy's pieces. Big Alan followed with a tough but convincing win and put his team up 2—0. Dayton's first board however sported an expert rating and Greg had been outplayed badly in the opening.

Greg grasped at anything he could and calculated a weird sacrifice that would leave him with nothing versus a bishop and a pawn. However, the extra pawn was a rook pawn and the bishop that remained had the opposite color on the queening square. Greg remembered this hideous formation was a guaranteed draw from one of Jim's lessons. He set out for it and the Dayton player grunted with frustration. The game was a draw and Greg sewed up the chance for the Eskimos to play for the title.

Jeff saw his team gain the match point and this took all the pressure off him. He focused deeply on his game with no worry. Jim saw fury in his eyes as this kid wanted to remain undefeated. The Dayton player was quite an experienced player and fought off Jeff's attacks one after another. Jeff continued the extreme tactical pressure and finally after a tiny mistake he inflicted damage to the opposing army. The Dayton player tipped over his king and offered a handshake, which Jeff accepted and giggled with pride. Escanaba had beat the high-powered Dayton team by the score of 3.5—.5 and had all the momentum going into the last round.

Flint won their match easily, but concern showed on the Dillards' faces. They knew they were better than Escanaba, but they realized Esky's supernatural momentum could be a huge problem. Terry had the resolve to play well in such circumstances, but the other Flint players looked dazed and already mentally defeated. Normally Flint got all the attention, but today everyone talked about the impressive Escanaba team. The Dillards left for lunch with their team and planned a desperation strategy along the way.

The Eskimos also set out for lunch. They didn't have a lot of time and they ate fast. All the while Jim filled them with easy tips to remember. Mostly though he continued to tell them to be the tougher team.

They returned to the site and everyone else in the room watched on as the exciting underdogs from the little Upper Peninsula prepared to take on the giants from Flint. The air roared with anticipation and Jim couldn't remember such a vibrant chess tournament in all his life. This was it, the moment of truth for his team.

Flint sat down at the table first, their blue and yellow expensive shirts standing out. The Eskimos followed. The sets and clocks were in place and although over a hundred other people occupied the room, the Eskimos only saw the Flint players and their coach. Greg and Big Alan had the Black pieces while Jeff and Tyler had the White side this round. The tournament director gave a final announcement and then set the championship round into motion.

Dillard Senior came over to Jim and offered a handshake this time. "Nice job Jim, you made it to the top." Jim accepted his greeting and Dillard Senior let go of his freezing hand at once. "My gosh, you're worried aren't you?" Jim glanced at him with ire. "Well you should worry, all we have to do is win two games and we'll beat you on tie-breaks. Wouldn't that be interesting?" Realizing Dillard Senior was right, his worried legs tried to carry him away, but the man pursued him. "Plus we have a surprise for you on boards one and three which should pretty much guarantee our points. Haven't had to use this trick in awhile, but watch and learn."

Jim did watch and he couldn't believe it when he saw Terry Dillard and the kid on Board 3 open with an insane gambit called the 'Grob'. Jim froze in place, they hadn't had time to study this opening properly and Greg and Big Alan were frozen also. They stood in brand new territory. He kicked himself in his mind. How could he have been so stupid to not cover that at least a little bit? They did have some time this morning to practice it and now it was too late.

Greg looked up and glanced back and Jim. He gave a look of bewilderment. Jim made a fist and pounded it lightly on his chest twice and then he nodded. He wasn't sure if his player could understand it or not, but it meant to fight for your life and don't give up. Big Alan had extreme difficulty. He burned almost an hour on his first four moves and played like he was lost in a jungle of complication.

Jeff and Tyler held even games, but they could see the dismay and confusion in their teammate's eyes and started to feel uneasy. Flint's plan worked to perfection and the Eskimos had been rattled. Whatever momentum they carried into the round had been totally extinguished by the clever Flint team.

Slowly Big Alan's game started to deteriorate. He had no time left to think and his opponent clearly outplayed him to a solid advantage in the opening. He didn't resign, but he took a pounding like he'd never been given in chess before. Dillard Senior gave Jim a glance that meant the match basically belonged to Flint.

Jeff on the other hand kept the Eskimos alive. He delivered an ingenious decoy tactic that just baffled his opponent. It was more of a trap than forced, but it had the proper timing and the effect Jeff wanted. He schooled his opponent the rest of the game and tied the match back up at one game each.

Tyler also showed extreme resolve and Jeff's energy flowed to him. Tyler had dropped a pawn and then regained it. His drive had been so forthright he snapped off another pawn and soon he had a won endgame. He looked back at Jim and then executed a winning move. The Flint player resigned and Dillard Senior immediately went over to him and chewed him out for violating the team's golden rule.

The Eskimos held the lead 2—1, but Jim's heart sank, because of the tiebreak situation. The Escanaba team was at a disadvantage and although they were guaranteed of tying for first place, unless Greg could pull off a draw or better, it was as good as losing.

Greg fought with relentless resolve. He didn't quit and he pushed his mind as hard as he could push it. Terry though seemed to have an answer for every move he made. The position became quite clear that Greg didn't know how to handle this opening properly. The mistakes he made Terry just gobbled up and Greg paid dearly. Hour after hour rolled by and the game continued. All the other games had been completed and now this last game; the championship game, would ultimately decide the state title.

Everyone, including the tournament director crowded around the board to see how it would end. They kept quiet, but a few whispers went back and forth by kibitzers. The director quieted them, but he didn't need to, both players tuned everything out but chess. Move after move Terry continued to hold his lead over Greg until the position started costing material. Greg went down a pawn, and then another. However, a rook remained on the board and with that, a miniscule chance at a draw. Terry just ran his assault in a forward direction.

Jim didn't watch too much, but finally couldn't resist and stole a peek. He didn't even spend half a minute on the position and his heart dropped with despair. He walked back to an open area in the room and sat by Jeff who seemed to know the same thing.

"It's over isn't it?" Jeff asked.

"I'm afraid so, I could beat Greg blindfolded in that position. And if I can do it, Terry Dillard can do it."

Jeff got up and pulled at his hair in anger and lightly pushed Jim. He cursed a few choice bad words and left the room in a rage. Jim chased after him.

"Jeff, don't leave," Jim tried to calm him.

"You're an idiot, how come you can't win the big game. This is insane. You should have prepared them for the 'Grob'. This is your fault. I would have crushed that jerk with that junk opening. I told you I should have been on first board," he hollered.

The anger in Jeff's eyes pierced him and he couldn't get any words out of his mouth. His head buzzed with what he was witnessing and a mild case of shock overtook him. The game had ended and the Flint players congratulated each other. The rest of the Eskimos came out of the room in astonishment at what had happened. The tournament director rounded everyone up for the trophy ceremony and Jim just wanted to break out in tears.

He fought the urge though and regained his composure and then had the group round Jeff up for trophies before it got too late. He felt like an 80 year old man and didn't want to suffer through this at all, but his inner self told him to get through this regardless. They tied for first, with the best team in the state. The accomplishment was tremendous. Something they should be proud of, not ashamed.

Just as Jeff's name had been called the other players got him into the room. He had won a large trophy for the best second board in the state and he seemed to calm instantly as the shiny hardware item was handed to him. Tyler took second best fourth board honors and received a nice sized trophy himself.

They waited a little longer and then were presented with the second place team trophy. Nobody smiled except for Craig when they took the picture. Jim tried to be cheerful, but the defeat dragged at him. Here it was 16 years later and the same haunting nightmare just repeated itself. Now he had a problem of disrespect by one of his players. The whole thing hurt, his mind was numb. Everything around him seemed surreal. He just couldn't believe they were outfoxed in the end by Flint. Now his poor players were to suffer the same misery he carried with him his whole life. This just wasn't right, how could things go so wrong so fast? What would it take to beat the Dillards?

The Escanaba team packed their bags and loaded the van. Jeff clung to his trophy like it was his best friend, while Tyler carried both his board trophy and the team trophy. After some distance in the van, all the players except Jeff started to snap out of the lapse. They even talked positive and started to realize what a huge accomplishment they had made. After a mere six months of playing chess, they were the second best team in the state of Michigan. An unbelievable feat, everyone back home would be so proud of them.

Jim and Jeff nonetheless, remained isolated from the group. Jeff's tirade burned at Jim and it stung. Jeff's anger had subsided somewhat, but he mildly voiced his complaints the whole way back and Jim couldn't wait for the ride to be over. He felt sick of hearing how he should have been on first board and Greg shouldn't have been. It didn't matter; they were destined to lose either way, because they didn't have the right chemistry to produce the win. Walters was right after all. He sensed the team would come up short and they did. They made a great run, but they were not a magical chess championship team. They needed more maturity as a team if they were going to get back to the title round.

CHAPTER 12

▼

THE PAIN OF CHESS

Days passed by that turned into weeks. Summer nearly completed its cycle and Jim didn't do anything but work and go fishing. He didn't even practice chess at all with Greg. He told Ole Cookie he just didn't feel well. Ole Cookie knew to give him some space, the championship defeat was hard on the first year coach and he tried his best to create space for Jim to overcome it and get ready for the next year.

Jim had serious doubts about chess. After work almost every night he took a long boat ride, his best answer for stress relief. He'd pull out his fishing pole and then just drift for hours in the middle of the big lake. Every now and then he'd hook into a large walleye or an even bigger pike. The fish weren't what he was after though, he was after something else. Something he didn't seem to understand or even describe.

These horrible feelings haunted him from inside and he started to wonder what was wrong. Why did life seem to be so awkward? Why didn't he seem to fit in? He thought for sure a chess team was the answer. The whole process had made life exciting, fun and had given him feelings he had not possessed in a long time. Before the state tournament he had never felt wanted or needed. Still his mind felt that it was time to pursue something other than chess. Chess had so much anguish and contained too much pressure on his nerves. The game had left him with nothing other than a deep gash across his caring heart.

Walters tried to soothe Jim's pain the best he could in emails. He even coaxed Jim into taking another vacation and just resting for a couple weeks. He even paid all the household bills one month so Jim could enjoy a little extra spending money and have some fun. Nothing worked and Jim's funk lasted all summer.

One month had gone by into the new school year. The chess team players were all juniors in high school, but they heard nothing about club and began to wonder if they'd get things going. Old Cookie pestered Jim constantly about getting the year started. Jim didn't know what words to say and instead replied, "I don't know," and shrugged his shoulders in resignation.

Walters bugged him as well. He kept telling him he owed it to those kids to at least give them an explanation of why he wouldn't be coaching if he chose to give it up. However, he didn't tell Walters the full extent of the Jeff situation, for fear Walters might become unglued and get angry with the kid and him for not taking care of the situation on the spot. Jim ran from his problem and he knew he shouldn't, but he had no energy to keep the chess team alive. He had failed again; chess was over.

Another month had gone by and Thanksgiving approached with still no chess club or team. The players decided to meet themselves and discuss the problem. Jeff even attended the meeting, as the pain of losing last year had long worn off him. He was ready to exact a little revenge and win the state title for sure this year.

The group agreed that they should approach their coach at his house and ask him kindly to come back. They also agreed to promise to try harder this year and not lose the big match.

After work one night, Jim sat depressed in his easy chair and stared at a wall. A knock came at his door and he answered it. To his surprise he saw four of his players on the porch, while Jeff stood back on the sidewalk. Blood rushed to his head in a nervous flurry and no words left his mouth. He wanted to tell him how sorry he was for not preparing them for the unorthodox opening, but his lips wouldn't part. The group just looked at him for a minute and then Greg came forward.

"Mr. B, we're sorry we let you down. We'll beat Flint this year, just give us another chance," Greg said and looked back at his teammates. "Please be our coach?"

That did it, the beginning of tears burst trough Jim's eyes and he held up one finger and turned back into his house and went to the kitchen. The front door hung open letting cold air into the house while the players waited outside for him to come back. Guilt struck him and it burned in his stomach. He thought he might throw up, but the emotion was only mental, not physical. After grabbing some tissues, he wiped his eyes and rinsed a washcloth with cold water. He compressed it to his face several times and looked and felt much better.

He returned to the front door and words still refused to come out of his mouth, so he motioned for them to follow him through a light trail of snow around the backyard to the lake. The lake grew to be a safe haven for him. He knew he'd soon be able to talk out there. He entered his shed and pulled out enough lawn chairs for everybody to sit and he set them around the barbeque fire pit. Jeff stayed back by the sidewalk and just paced. The other players sat down in the chairs and waited while their coach went back into the house and came out with some marshmallows, graham crackers and chocolate bars.

Jim piled up some spare wood, lit a fire and didn't mutter a word. The boys just sat and waited. They seemed more relaxed. The fire took off well and warmed everyone up. Jim handed each young man a very long metal camping fork. Naturally they all grabbed marshmallows out of the bag and started to roast them over the fire.

Darkness had just begun and the boys mashed their soft marshmallows with the chocolate between the graham crackers and ate the treat with a smile. Jim had one of the treats himself and started to relax. He concentrated on taking deep breaths and finally his chest started to loosen up to where talking became possible again.

"I'm sorry I didn't prepare you guys for the 'Grob' attack. It's a unique opening that is pretty easy to get a good position from," Jim took a deep breath, "if you'd have seen it before. It was my fault, not your fault. I guess I have some bad luck to overcome somewhere."

Jeff became tired of waiting and inched closer and closer to the fire. Everyone noticed him, but paid him no mind. When he got close enough, he grabbed an extra chair and sat keeping his distance.

"Will you coach us again?" Greg asked.

"Do you guys really even want me back?" he asked them in a sincere manner and saw revelation take to their faces.

"Of course, why wouldn't we want you back, you're the greatest chess coach in the world," Greg answered for the group.

Jim's chest started to tighten again. Although he could barely do it, he forced himself to look each one of them in the eye. And what he saw was that they all stared back, even Jeff meant business here. After making himself take a deep breath, he put another marshmallow on his fork and twirled it in the fire. The players waited with endurance for him to make a decision.

Jim's mind had realized an important thing. The chess team had become more than Jim Berzchak. It had become an entity or life form of its own. He deduced that the problems with Jeff were far from over. Even scarier thoughts plagued him that it truly was impossible for this team to win a state championship with Jeff in his current state. The kid would either have to change and learn to become respectful or leave the team. This challenge appeared impracticable, but Jim felt he must continue forward with the program he had started. Win or lose it was him now that had to be the toughest person.

"I sort of let you guys down," Jim pushed the words out.

"No," Tyler said and the other players followed his word.

"Yes, I did. I gave up mentally. I wasn't the toughest coach. I was weak. We should not be dwelling on our loss, I ask you guys for your forgiveness on that."

"Mr. B, don't worry about it," Greg assured.

"Yes, Greg I need to apologize. I probably didn't do anything wrong to anyone per se, but I ran from a problem here and for that I'm sorry."

"Well, we forgive you," Craig added. He hoped the chess program still existed.

"All right guys," Jim continued. He started to feel renewed. "There will be some changes I'm sure. I am going to make stronger decisions." He paused and saw the relieved looks in their eyes. "It won't be easy but I promise I will be fair." He looked them in the eyes. "Chess practice will start back up in two weeks. We will have a ton of work to do."

The players celebrated by bumping their fists and shouting some loud hoots and hollers. Jim prompted them to be quieter as to not disturb the neighbors, but they continued to celebrate. Even Jeff looked relieved but Jim squared him in the eye for the first time and gave the young man a silent but clear message. He'd give him one more chance to be a team player or it was over. Disrespect on this chess team would no longer be tolerated.

CHAPTER 13

▼

A SAD GOODBYE

The practices began and the team went into overtime to catch up for lost efforts. Negaunee was first on the list for the league and the Eskimos knew they would have to whip themselves into proper shape in order to not have a serious letdown. Jim made charts, photocopied books, gave them articles, and drilled them with every chess lesson he had.

Although the team's progress was nothing short of phenomenal, they still didn't click right. Jim stood amazed one evening after the team had left the club meeting and just shook his head. They certainly had twice the strength as the previous year and yet they didn't seem to form that union that every team needs in order to play their absolute best. He questioned himself that maybe they would get so good they could overcome this type of problem. However, every time he rationalized this scenario a picture of Walters entered into his mind and shook his finger. The game should not be about winning or losing, but having a good time and playing tough. He didn't know how to get rid of Jeff's tension and bring him in unison with the rest of the team.

The team got past Negaunee, but tripped against Marquette by losing one of the matches. Greg did not play well because he had the flu and the team had a difficult time executing good chess. Burnout seemed to creep into their attitudes and even though they held the power, they made flat moves that didn't win.

To make matters worse, Jeff started to insist on becoming first board. In all fairness after the team split another match, this time with West Iron County, Jim agreed that alternatives needed to be looked at. Negaunee had pulled into a first place tie with them and the two teams were destined to meet each other in the last match of the season. The winner of course, laid a clear path to States, while the loser was going to stay home.

Greg had faltered a bit against other teams and it was time for him to either show his strength in head to head competition and keep the first board position or give it up to Jeff. Jim decided a three game match best decided who would get the top spot and one game would be played each day after school until a winner had emerged.

The rules for Greg and Jeff's match were simple. Best of three games, game in 60-minute time control and if the match resulted in a tie, Greg would have the advantage and keep first board since he currently held the higher rank. The players agreed to this setup and Jeff looked relieved to finally get his long awaited crack at the top spot.

The first game he came out with fire and just smoked Greg using the Four Pawn's Attack in a line of the King's Indian Defense. He shattered Greg's defenses from the onset and when the game ended, he stood up and pointed a long finger at his coach and said, "I told you I was better than him."

"Hold on," Greg answered back. "Match isn't quite over yet. Another game tomorrow."

Jeff just waved him off and left. However, Greg went home and planned a surprise for him the next day after school. He had worked on a trap all evening long. He even neglected his homework to dedicate his whole night towards a unique line to play, some sort of complication that even Jeff didn't have the ability to cope with. After a few searches on the internet and some computer analysis, he honed his skill in the variation he'd attempt to steer the game into. The next day when the two played, he sprung his novel idea. Although Jeff fought as brilliantly as he could and even stayed away from some real problems Greg posed at him, he ultimately remained one move behind the whole game. Once Greg's sharp endgame kicked in, Jeff knew he was going to get ground down move by move and he tipped his king over. Jim gave him a serious look about resigning like that, but Jeff left the room before any complaints were registered.

Jim sat down and prepared to look the game over with Greg when Jeff's head popped back into the room. "Tomorrow you're mine, I'm going to win this match," he hollered and left again.

Jim complemented Greg on his wonderful game and his unique trap. Even against a solid tournament veteran, this line had some merit and he recommended that Greg keep that pet variation under his lid and work on it from time to time.

School let out the next day and the two players met for their final match game. They had to wait a half an hour for Jim to get off work and arrive at the school. They didn't say a word to each other and remained quiet until their coach came into the room. Once Jim got settled he wished them each the best of luck on such an important game and that no matter what, each player had played great. He instructed them to start and they did.

Unlike the first two games, this one took a passive course. Greg didn't risk an aggressive game this time. Jeff had too much skill on him there. Instead he chose the quiet Stonewall Defense and waited Jeff out. Clearly irritated by such a slow choice of openings, Jeff tried to turn the tables and make the game wild. Jim questioned some of his moves, but they were clever and held many pitfalls for Greg to stumble on. Greg refused to budge. He set up a wall of pawns for defense and just waited for his opponent to come forward. Every chance he got to trade a piece evenly, he did. The game played on and on. Greg started to get into time trouble, but the position remained easy to assess and Jeff found it difficult to penetrate the wall.

Slowly the pieces started to come off the board one by one. Jeff tried to keep the queens on the board so he could attack, but he soon realized that if he didn't trade queens even up, he would lose a pawn. Next he found his rooks in the same bargain and traded them evenly too. The position came down to bishops of opposite color with four pawns each. Jim noted in his mind how drawish the game looked despite the two players continuing to fight it out.

More pawns started to come off the board until they only had their bishop and one pawn each. Understanding a draw was as good as a win, Greg sacrificed his bishop for Jeff's remaining pawn. Such a move was absurd to do in a regular position, but in this case it guaranteed Greg's draw because a bishop and king alone are not enough to force checkmate. Greg had successfully retained the first board position on the team.

Upset, Jeff just shook his head in disgust. He did manage to walk out of the room in a calm manner without saying a single word. Jim and Greg both heard a loud smash against a locker and then another.

"He must be really mad he lost, to punch a locker like that hey?" Jim asked Greg. "I wish he wouldn't act that way."

"He's certainly got some issues," Greg whispered.

"You said it. Nice match Greg, you really showed some heart. I am extremely proud of how you played. You know if you keep it up, you could end up a master some day."

"Thanks Mr. B, I just hope we can get to States. Since second place doesn't get to go this year because of all the budget cut talks, I'm a little worried."

"Me and you both. I'm not sure we can justify or convince the school of letting us use the van if we're a second place team, no matter how good we are." Jim paused as he looked up to the classroom clock. It read 5:00 PM exactly. The same chill that ran down his back when Walters left on the plane last winter did the same thing again. The feeling made him quite uncomfortable. "I better go Greg," he said with concern. He packed the chess gear up and went out the school at a half jog.

A pungent metal taste filled his mouth when he got into his Mustang and he drove it on the ice-covered roads. He felt in such a rush to get home, all the while he couldn't figure out why he was in such a hurry. The car almost lost control several times and when he swerved and just missed a parked car by inches he took several deep breaths and did his best to calm down from a growing panic attack. Fortunately he only had a few blocks left to drive and he soon pulled the car into the garage and closed the door behind it.

The furnace kicked on inside the house and Jim took off his coat and placed it on the rack. Still chilled, he covered up on the couch with a blanket and decided to watch some television. He continued to feel panicked and didn't understand why. He didn't have to work the next day, chess was taken care of until the Negaunee match, Jeff's goofiness really didn't bother him much anymore and the spare time in between should have afforded him some badly needed leisure.

With his finger he clicked on the big screen television and started to flick through the channels. When he got to the national channels he saw that a live broadcast from all the major networks dominated the airtime. There had been some sort of terrorist attack in the Middle East and he didn't feel like paying it any attention. While trying to find a cable station with no news, he continued to feel chilled to his bones. He stopped what he was doing and got up to turn up the heat. After adjusting the thermostat, warm waves of air poured out of the vents into the house and he returned to his spot on the couch. To his astonishment the television screen flashed to a helicopter view of a naval ship with smoke coming out of it in several places.

Jim froze when he saw the caption, 'LIVE—PERSIAN GULF—U.S.S. RID-DICK SEA.' With his thumb he cranked the volume, his eyes mesmerized.

"Now, explain this again Tom, one more time for our viewers," he heard a newscaster say.

"Sure Donna. It appears that just minutes ago terrorists have attacked a U.S. naval ship pulling out of port on its way home after a long tour of duty in the Persian Gulf. Allegedly the suicidal terrorists faked a plea for help in a smaller boat and gained entrance to the ship by using guns and carrying a large home-made bomb. It is reported that the captain of the ship was able to trick the terrorists into detonating the bomb in a non-essential portion of the ship. The damage was immense, but surprisingly none of the ship's regular crew at all was hurt. However, it is widely speculated the heroic deed may have cost the captain his own life in the process. The captain's body, nor the bodies of the terrorists are yet to be recovered at this time as far as we know."

"Wow, Tom sounds like this captain handled matters with unusual tact."

"Yes Donna, I don't know what the military process is for awarding bravery, but you have to figure they're going to hand out some medals for this one, even if it may be posthumously. Quite a stalwart display, I just don't know what else to say, other than I feel for the captain's family and friends."

Paralyzed Jim couldn't move. The television switched off to other announcers, but he remained still. He knew right away that it was Walter's ship they were talking about and that he was the captain.

An hour passed and he still did not move. On and off he cried not understanding what had happened. He broke his trance for a minute and tried to phone Walter's mother, but there was no answer. He tried again and no answer. He sat back down and mulled over the impossible information he had processed.

For two days he did not sleep one minute. The match with Negaunee approached and Walter's mother still could not be reached. He had called in sick at work yet again and by now his awesome track record of good attendance had been used up. The cafeteria manager started to become upset that his work ethic was not what it had been, but decided to let it slide one more time.

Jim watched the news day and night and researched everything he could on the internet. Although the situation looked bleak for Walters, they never once mentioned his name or actually confirmed the death of the captain. He still did not get through to Walter's mother on the phone either and worry set in.

Not totally sure how to handle the situation, he assumed that everything would be fine and that the whole thing was maybe misreported or somehow it was the wrong ship or something. With some repair to his confidence, he gathered his team for their big match with Negaunee. Ole Cookie had an extra day off and decided to attend the big league clinching match for the Eskimos and to see if Jim needed any help.

When the team gathered before the match, Jim talked to his players and they immediately noticed the distress and hurt in his red eyes.

"What's wrong Mr. B?" Greg asked.

"Nothing, we just gotta get past Negaunee today," he replied. "Even if we fundraise, I don't think we'll get any support to go to States if we don't win this match. They're only letting one team go to States this year, the league winning team. We gotta get past them."

"Darn right, we're taking that state title this year," Jeff piped up with confidence.

"Okay guys, we've never lost to this team. Let's just take care of these guys in high fashion and win that state title in a couple of weeks. Be tougher than them."

"Darn right, Flint is going down in a couple weeks," Jeff added.

The Eskimos settled into their chairs while Craig got his pad of paper and pen out to record the results of the match. All the players except for Jeff looked mentally shaken. Something was wrong with their coach and inside they could feel whatever sorrow ailed him. The match started and the games began.

In the first game, Jeff came out with his patented first win, which was followed by a quick win from Greg. Things started to look good right from the beginning. However, Big Alan and Tyler didn't have any gusto in their play and the Negaunee bottom boards stayed firm and won, keeping things even at a score of 2-2 and a first match draw.

Neither team budged on giving up first place, but Jim relaxed a little when he saw the tie-breaks sway into Escanaba's favor for once. All they had to do was get two more points and they would be heading to States. The Esky players were not happy with the draw, but showed no urgency either. The road seemed simple enough to follow and they assumed they could easily get past Negaunee one more time.

"It's all right," Jim stated before the second match started. "We're not having a great match. We got the tie-breaks though this time, we'll get past them. They aren't half as tough as a Flint team. This shouldn't be bad. Just play tough."

The team reassembled in their chairs and so did Negaunee. They started the next round and again, it was Jeff who embarrassed his opponent to give the Eskimos a one-point lead. But, to Escanaba's dismay, Big Alan and Tyler were flat again. Tyler's opening plan had been misplayed and he found himself a pawn down, while Big Alan struggled miserably in a complicated position. Greg held an even line of defense that kept his game equal. More moves went by and

Negaunee tied the score on fourth board when Tyler got checkmated. Big Alan barely held out for a draw and this result lifted Greg who only had to draw now instead of win to keep States alive. His position was solid, with no advantages, but no deficiencies and he felt great about holding Escanaba's team edge.

A few moves went by and then the Negaunee player to everyone's surprise played a trick move. By luck he stumbled onto a line of play that caused tremendous complications. He sacked a bishop for two of Greg's pawns and then pushed one to the seventh rank almost as if by accident. Greg's face went pale and he couldn't seem to stop the opposing player's pawn from turning into a queen. Every continuation he drummed up for a defense left him down in serious material. Finally, after 10 more moves of the game, the Negaunee player queened his pawn and won the game with a checkmate. This gave Negaunee the match win by the score of 2.5—1.5 for their first ever defeat of Escanaba.

The whole room fell quiet as the stunning upset entered the consciousness of all the people present. The room stayed silent for a solid minute until the Negaunee players emerged from their trance and started to celebrate. Escanaba's loss was real this time, they blew a match they should have won. Jim shook the hand of Negaunee's coach and congratulated him on a fine win and then turned around to console his team.

"Guys it's okay, we had…" Jim was interrupted as Jeff slapped a hand across the side of Greg's head.

Immediately Jim stepped in between the two players and took one of Jeff's fists to his nose. Blood started to drain out of his left nostril and dizziness took his mind. Ole Cookie grabbed Jeff and wrestled him to the floor. He pinned Jeff's shoulders and hollered at him to calm down. Curse after curse flew out of Jeff's mouth. Only after a few minutes of Ole Cookie's strong arms holding him down did he decide to listen to the coaches. Negaunee's coach went over to aid Ole Cookie and together they were able to get control of the physical part of the situation.

"I told you a hundred times I should have been on first board!" Jeff shouted. "He's just like our dumb coach, he always loses the big game."

"Just be quiet," Ole Cookie warned.

"Stupid coaches, stupid players. Now I'm not going to win a state title this year, and it's all because of these idiots."

The words stung at Jim's insides, but his face had real hurt as well. Anger took him. His mind told him at this moment Walters was gone for good. A strange feeling empowered him with strength and he glared at Jeff.

"You're kicked off the team. I'm sorry it ended this way, but you'll never play for me again."

Jeff laughed, "you'll never win without me, I'm the strongest player you've got. I'm the only one who knows how to win around here." He broke loose of Ole Cookie's grip and left the room in a huff.

"Jeff," Jim called before he crossed the doorway. The kid turned back and looked. "What have I always said? It's not about winning or losing. It's about how tough you play. Yeah, maybe you yourself are a winning machine, but we always lose as a team because of your crummy attitude. Don't ever come back to this team again until you learn how to behave."

Jeff grumbled and stormed out of the school. Jim checked over Greg who was fine and then he wiped his own nose with a tissue and cleaned up. The physical damage to his face was minimal. He finally went over to Negaunee's coach and team and congratulated them all one more time to break the horrible scene they had just witnessed. The Negaunee players showed mutual understanding and compassion and then wasted no time in leaving.

Jim returned his attention to the rest of his players and calmed them down. He reassured his team that things would be better. He then nodded to Ole Cookie and mentioned that an impromptu pizza party was in order.

"Why are we having a pizza party Mr. B? We can't celebrate a loss. We didn't earn the right to go to States, let alone win it, did we?" Tyler asked, demoralized from his terrible play.

"I don't know if we'll ever win a state title Tyler," he said shrugging his shoulders. He looked all his players in the eyes. "I do know though, this is one darn tough chess team. I'm glad you guys have played your absolute best for me. I'm also extremely proud of each and every one of you, no matter how much we win or how much we lose." The team smiled, but Jim lifted a finger into the air, "Well I'm also kind of hungry, I haven't eaten in about three days." The kids laughed at what seemed to be dry humor and he curled a half smile in return. He didn't let on that his words were the total truth.

CHAPTER 14

▼

IN THE DOLDRUMS

Spring passed and the summer air warmed Lake Michigan. Jim had pulled in from a boat ride and went into the house to check his mail. Delivery had left a chess magazine in his mailbox and he noticed the results of the state championship had been printed. The headline read 'Tune-Heads from Poly-Science-Tech Score Perfect Championship'. On the cover showed a picture of a team he had never seen before, a group of tall, pale young men all wearing big smiles and headphones on their ears. They had no coach, but their players huddled in a circle around their championship trophy.

Inside, the article told how the Poly-Sci team scored an unprecedented perfect score in state high school team chess. Other information indicated that their school refused to pay for a coach, so the players took the burden amongst themselves and they honed their skills using the internet. The most intriguing part of their team was that they all had musical talent of some sorts and they liked to listen to classical songs while playing chess. Jim thought this to be kind of strange, but admitted that even he himself was fond of listening to the harmonies of Bach while practicing at home from time to time. The argument of people using music to help sooth one's nerves didn't seem totally absurd to him either and the rhythm probably aided in concentration.

He saw pictures of the other teams and in second place was the Flint team. They all wore scowls on their faces. Dillard Senior looked distraught while he clutched his patented statistic taking laptop in his arms. Even though the picture was black and white, the red in his face showed from anger. Terry Dillard didn't look too happy either, as Josh Marin the first board from Poly-Sci had clearly schooled him. The game score was printed under the best games section and Jim thoroughly enjoyed the newcomer's tactical brilliance.

At the very bottom of the list of teams and their scores he saw the Negaunee squad. No trophy, no honorable mention, they didn't even win a match. Jim felt though they probably had a wonderful trip and memories to hold for a lifetime. He just wished things had gone different for the Eskimos. However, as delighted as he was to see Flint get their butt kicked, a new dilemma struck him when he saw the Poly-Sci team's statistics. They consisted of sophomores and freshmen and undoubtedly would be seeking a defense to their impressive title run next year.

"Nothing like having an even bigger giant to throw us around," Jim muttered to himself. "Gosh, we have all we can handle with Flint, where did this Poly-Science team come from?" He dropped the magazine onto a coffee table and then looked up. "I know Walters, be the toughest team, it's not about winning. I got it."

*   *   *   *

The summer had nearly ended and Jim had not had a comfortable night of sleep. Work started to get rough for him. The management had enough of his excuses and only Ole Cookie who picked up his extra slack kept him from getting fired. Most days he just went for boat rides on the lake and then called in sick. He had finally been in touch with Walter's mother and she confirmed everything he knew all along, that Walters had most likely died in the blast on his ship. Sure the body was never recovered, but after six months now and not a word, the outlook certainly looked bleak.

Depression gripped him hard and the only thing that seemed to pull him out of it were summer lessons to his four players. They kept him up to date and kept him on a forward track. On exceptionally tough days he made his mind focus solely on his players, to give them everything they deserved in a coach. That meant he had to keep his thoughts on a direct course of chess and coaching.

Greg and Ole Cookie came over for practice one afternoon and broke fresh news to him about Jeff. The other players had said that his legal guardian landed a good paying job out west and that they had moved. Evidently the rumors were that Jeff had known for some time about his move and now in hindsight everything showed quite clear. His behavior resulted in his last chance to win a state title with this school and when it ended without the top prize he got quite bent out of shape over it. That was the reason he flew off the handle so badly after the Negaunee defeat. Jeff knew he'd never be an Eskimo again, whether a champion or not.

Jim felt bad and even had some regret. Not under the most favorable of circumstances was Jeff ever coming back. Not that he would have been allowed to anyway, but the finality of it struck Jim hard. Still he focused his mind and decided that he'd work with his players at full capacity. Even though Craig could not even come close to filling the gap Jeff left behind, he'd do everything possible to get his Eskychess-Express back on the tracks and moving forward. This time with no pressure on the players to win, they only had to play tough and enjoy.

After the conversation, Jim showed Greg a valuable lesson on rook and pawn endgames. When it all ended, Ole Cookie packed up Greg's chess gear and Jim walked them to their car and bid them a good evening. He turned to go back inside when a black colored Sedan pulled up and two men in blue military uniforms got out. The men were well decorated with different types of medals and ribbons pinned to their chests. One held a long brown box and the other a flag. Jim's stomach started to get sick immediately, but his inner strength kept his emotions in place.

"Good afternoon sir," one of them spoke, "I am Admiral Tompkins of the United States Navy." The two men approached Jim and he felt paralyzed and his breathing felt forced. "Are you James L. Berzchak?"

"Yes," Jim half whispered.

"On behalf of the United States Navy, we are saddened to give you the news that your friend Captain Junior E. Walters has passed, in a combat situation. I would like to present you with this flag of the United States to remember him by and as a symbol to show his dedication and…" the admiral paused briefly, "his ultimate sacrifice that he gave for his country. It may seem like little compensation now, but he was truly a hero." The admiral handed Jim the flag and took a controlled step backwards and the other man with less decoration, holding the box stepped forward.

"I have a package here for you," he stated in quiet but forced fashion. "Captain Walters had this in a storage unit we allow for our officers. Your name and address are current and we legally are delivering it to you." He handed the box over. "We also have information and death certificates to collect your life insurance check—"

"Life insurance!" Jim exclaimed not quite knowing where the energy came from. "No, no, no. He has a mother and a sister, with kids no less. I can't take that."

Both men smiled. This was not their first 'death news' assignment and they always felt amused when someone had life insurance coming and didn't know it. The admiral gave a hand motion, while the other man handed Jim a manila envelope and explained.

"Well, I'm not supposed to say this," he looked at the admiral who nodded for him to proceed, "but they were very well cared for. Captain Walters evidently was a fanatic about investing and insurance. We delivered their military insurance information before we came here. Trust me his mother and sister are well off and their needs are taken care of and then some. Please do not worry about them. Captain Walters was an excellent provider."

Jim only peeked a little bit, but could see the long digits of $200,000 inside and his chest deflated.

"There are also papers in there for this house I believe. It is now legally yours without tax or penalty due to Captain Walter's death in a combat zone. His mother expressed that she wanted you to have his share because her and her daughter are choosing to move to Georgia soon to live closer to some other relatives."

The military men didn't stay much longer and consoled Jim one more time. Then they left as rapidly as they had arrived.

Jim went back into the house and sorted through the documents. He remained controlled and awed at the claim information for $200,000—untaxed. The amount was staggering and at the same time depressing. He'd tear it up in a second and move back to his old apartment for ten more minutes with his best friend, but reality checked him. His breathing started to normalize and he relaxed. Amazement still gripped him at how Walters had suddenly made his life of constant struggle and toil, into one of productivity and leisure. Through Walter's sacrifice he had been given a precious gift and he knew he had better not waste it.

The phone rang and captured his attention by surprise. Ole Cookie was on the line.

"Jeez, they just called me to see if I knew if you were coming in today," he bellowed. "Jim do you want to get fired or what?"

Calm and with a sense of peace Jim replied, "Cookie, don't take this the wrong way, but I think I'm done working at the cafeteria. It was good to me, but it's over."

"Over! Over!" Ole Cookie replied with excitement. "How the heck are you going to pay your bills? You can't quit, you need this job, Jim please come to your senses."

"It's okay Cookie. I promise I'm not delusional. This time everything is well taken care of. I have a friend in a high place," he said and hung up the phone softly.

He then picked up the box and shook it. It rattled and he couldn't tell what was inside, maybe a brick for all he knew. Snug, he put the box in a cabinet and left it alone. Whatever secret it contained he'd save for another day. Another day when he'd need to draw strength from his best friend who was now gone forever.

CHAPTER 15

▼

A MESSAGE FROM ABOVE

August rolled on and the heat combined with humidity made life quite uncomfortable. Normally the breeze off the lake was more than enough to squelch a hot spell, but this day Jim felt like having some air conditioning and decided to purchase a small unit at the shopping center.

The cool air relaxed him and he was even able to take a nap. His sleep had been horrible all summer long and if his body frame wasn't thin enough already, he had lost another 10 pounds. The insurance check was delivered and cashed the day it arrived and Jim had lived without his job now for a couple weeks. He promised himself that he'd get new employment soon, but having more than enough money in the bank to meet his needs, he didn't make time to do that. He had it made, yet with all the wonders Walters had provided for him, he wasn't happy and his problems were merely masked, not solved. Deep down he knew this was not good.

His chess had been non-existent as well. The last chess thing he remembered was that weird 'Tune-Head' team sweeping states. When he awoke from his nap he noticed a chess magazine on the floor. The mere thought of playing chess just tired him. The advertisement for the Michigan Open showed in big block letters and drew his attention rather easy. His tie with Dillard Senior a couple years back made him even more ill on chess and he decided to get up and make a cup of tea to sip on. When he finished his drink, he noticed another strange thing in the cabinet. The box the men had sent from Walters leaned along the edge of the door like it had been tipped over.

"Walters, you aren't playing with me are you?" he called into the empty house.

Weak from the lack of nutrition, he pulled out the box. He stared at it for several minutes and began to grieve for his friend once more. The mystery of it burned inside him and in a fit of anger, he tore the box open and pulled out the contents. When he saw what it was, he set it down on his couch and took a calm step backwards. The item was a trophy he had seen a long time ago only once. It was caked with dust and the king at the top had a broken cross that had been glued back together. He reached over and pushed his thumb across the plate and it began to brighten. The words at the bottom read: BEST 2nd BOARD— MICHIGAN HIGH SCHOOL STATE TEAM CHESS CHAMPIONSHIP— 1989.

"Oh my gosh," Jim said to himself, "this is what he was talking about, I can't believe it."

In the box he also noticed a small note and picked it up and read it.

BERZCHAK—WELL IF YOU'RE READING THIS, SOMETHING PROBABLY WENT TERRIBLY WRONG AND I'M NOT HERE ANYMORE. I PULLED THIS TROPHY OUT OF THE GARBAGE AT STATES. I WOULD LIKE YOU TO DISPLAY IT AND BE PROUD OF IT. YOU WERE OUR M.V.P. THAT YEAR, DON'T EVER FORGET THAT. DON'T LET OUR TECHNICALITY OF LOSING THE TITLE DRAG ON YOUR FUTURE. YOU WERE THE REAL STRENGTH OF OUR TEAM AND YOU INSPIRED ME TO GREAT HEIGHTS NOT ONLY IN CHESS—ALSO IN LIFE. YOU WERE THE BEST FRIEND I EVER HAD. YOUR FRIEND AND YOUR BROTHER—WALTERS

He folded the note and put it back in the box. Tears streamed down his face. He gave the trophy a quick shine and placed it on the mantle for permanent display. A good feeling took him. Although he felt weak still, he grabbed the chess magazine and examined the advertisement for the Michigan Open. He knew Ole Cookie had to work this weekend and that Greg wouldn't be able to make it. The solitude would certainly do him better. After understanding the tournament was held in the same place as previous years, he packed his bag, grabbed his wallet and hopped into his Mustang. Finally, he felt like playing some chess.

*   *   *   *

Jim checked into the same hotel and the same room he and Walters had stayed in just two short years before at the same tournament. In the morning he went to breakfast and managed to force himself to eat food. The process made him nauseous but he new he lacked serious strength and the energy would be badly needed later, especially for the last round. He made his way into the tournament hall, signed his entry form and paid his fees. The tournament director looked excited to see him, because both Dillards had also entered along with Poly-Sci's all star Josh Marin. This group held 'powerhouse' status and the event promised to be nothing short of exceptional.

"Glad to see you're back after a year of absence Jim," the tournament director said. "Where's your friend Walters?"

Jim saw both Dillards off to the side lift their eyes in concern. They knew they could beat Jim, but Walters, his potential presence drew their attention.

"He had a prior engagement," Jim replied in a slightly sarcastic manner. "He sent me here to win all my games this weekend for him." Jim grabbed 'Ticker' and while ignoring everybody he headed into the tournament room.

Dillards laughed at his comment, but they also had noticed a change in his personality. He appeared thin and frail like always and yet determination seemed to flow from his soul and appeared to give him unrecognized strength.

The first round started shortly after and Jim took care of a Class B player from Battle Creek. He didn't even pull out his mental board inside his mind. Just like Walters and much unlike his old self, he plowed through the guy with serious aggression. There was no rust on his playing ability and if anything, the break actually did him some good and made him even sharper. Dillards and Marin on the three boards above him noticed how quick Jim handled his opponent. However, they won their games in decisive fashion as well.

Round two had Jim on fourth board again and he just stunned an 1800 with a Smith-Morra Gambit. Jim had never played it before in competition, but walloped the poor fellow in 18 moves with a brilliant tactical setup. The top three boards followed suit and the intensity for a showdown of the top four started to build. Round three held the same results. Jim punished a 1900 badly after the man tried a weird idea on move five. The move was supposed to be a trap in theory and Jim pulled the game out of familiar territories and inflicted a voracious kingside attack that swallowed all of his opponent's pieces.

After the game Jim felt terribly ill and drained of all energy. He left the room and showed no interest in how any of the other games were going. He stopped at the hotel restaurant before retiring for the evening and forced himself to eat a steak dinner with baked potato, along with a glass of pop. When he filled up, he went back to his room and crashed on the bed. His mind stayed set for a few minutes of thought, that of being the only games that mattered this time were his. After a couple minutes everything went blank to the grasp of sleep.

In the morning he awoke in high spirits and freshly rested. Still, his stomach bothered him and he felt a slight headache pounding inside his brain. Eating breakfast was more trouble than he anticipated as well, but he forced his food down at the restaurant anyway to gain energy for later. Somewhat under the weather, he made his way to the tournament room and drew strength for battle from places his mind didn't even know existed. Again, like two years previous, the top boards just took an attitude of refusing to lose and Jim wasn't going to be the weak one this time.

He was paired against a pesky expert he had read about in the state chess magazine and remembered that the French Defense was his pet line. When the games started he deliberately went for the Exchange Variation to see what the guy had. Every move he made was consistent of what theory Jim had of the game. This guy really did know his French lines. The position became difficult to assess and Jim finally turned on the chess set in his mind and calculated variation after variation. The game seesawed back and forth when finally the expert played a move that clearly was not from the theory of the position. The expert's move was emotional and Jim's logic kicked in and he forced momentum strategically by saddling his opponent with two weak isolated rook-pawns. He then steered his king and rooks forward and drove for the kill. The expert didn't feel like playing out the lost endgame and resigned on the spot.

Dillards on boards one and three looked at him with newfound respect. That was not the same old Jim Berzchak that played out stale five-hour games on the fringe of equality. This guy resembled something more of a wrecking ball. Even Josh Marin on the second board, right below Dillard Senior seemed to have a twinkle of admiration in his eye.

Jim looked at the tournament report and although he was in first place he assumed that Dillards and Marin would all win their games also. In that scenario, he would play Marin on Board 2, while the Dillards would square off amongst each other on Board 1. He was quite dismayed that he wouldn't get the chance to play one of the Dillards, but he also figured now was the time to learn a thing or two about the young hot shot Josh Marin who seemed to be more absorbed in his music during his games than the actual playing of chess. Still if he could help Greg get any edge against this tactical genius, he'd take it. And the first edge would be to demonstrate how to be tough against this whiz kid.

With the extra time, Jim went back to his room. He felt like he had the flu and even vomited. He wasn't sure if he had a fever or not. After some rest he felt so weak he almost couldn't get up from the chair. The fifth and final round would start in less than 15 minutes and he knew he had to get down there to play his game. He forced himself up, grabbed 'Ticker' for one more brutal battle and then bought a clear soda pop to drench his parched throat. Whatever illness he had, his body ran rampant, but his mind stayed free. He thought about Larry Lodish and a smile took over on his face.

The top four players were tied for first place. All had perfect scores. As predicted the Dillards were paired on the first board while Jim matched up with Josh Marin on the second. The last round of the biggest tournament in Michigan was about to begin and the excitement was in the air. All the other players had eyes for the top two boards and wondered who would win the tournament.

Everyone found their places and Jim started 'Ticker' for his opponent's move. He held the Black pieces this game and Marin opened with his king pawn, an opening of aggression. Jim sat and wondered for a while. He wasn't sure if he should go aggressive, passive or somewhere in between. Everything he had seen up to this point by Marin, which wasn't saying much, had been all ultra aggressive. This kid came out like lightning and then knocked his opponents out cold. Remembering the final game Greg had played against Jeff in the battle for first board, he employed Greg's same idea. He set up a defensive wall of pawns and dared Marin to come and get him.

Marin indeed stepped up to the challenge. Every move he made was accurate and troublesome. Jim couldn't believe how much book theory this young man knew. Impressive was the only word to use. Still, Jim reinforced his pawn wall again, and again. He used his chess set in his mind sparingly, saving the energy for later and keeping the plan simple and logical. Marin continued to attack and on each and every reply, Jim defended. Move after move the hunt persisted. For hours the game continued in this fashion.

Jim started to feel what little energy he had left, fade away. Marin was actually wearing him down. Maybe it was a case of being in the fifth round, but the kid just didn't make any mistakes. For sure this youngster would end up an international master soon and if he kept at it, he'd most likely be a grandmaster someday, no problem.

On the 34th move Marin played a move Jim didn't expect. Jim just sat there and stared at the position. He felt sleepy and his head began to pound harder with pain. However, he pulled up his mental chessboard and forced it to crunch lines and variations. He had to save this game at all costs. He could feel Walter's presence, but yet couldn't see him. He focused even more on the board to find the right move.

After a while, a unique idea came to him. The whole thing was built on intuition, from a position he had remembered seeing in one of Emmanuel Lasker's old games. It required a pawn trade and then a sacrifice of a rook worth five points, for a knight and a pawn worth four points. The maneuver was deceptive and tricky to evaluate, any strong master could easily believe the position's assessment to be false by material count. The knight and pawn actually could untangle a few moves later and become a powerhouse threat. Jim got his board rolling in his mind. After a long deliberation he decided this course of action was about all he had left. Marin's regular game was too strong for him at this point and he needed to change the momentum somehow. He grabbed his rook, and took Marin's knight.

Marin slowly recorded the move with no emotion. Several minutes elapsed and he made his move and snapped up the rook. Again, he seemed like he was rolling to the music inside his head and didn't even seem worried about Jim's plan of attack.

Time was starting to run out for Jim and his energy now was lower than ever. The board in his mind blurred, no energy remained to think. He got up from the board and bought an apple juice from a vending machine and forced it down. He returned and tried to force his mind to calculate more variations, but it was no go. Intuition was all he had left.

His stomach felt ill, but nothing in the room came to his attention outside of the position at hand. His mind failed to see what to do. He could only feel that there was some small break in Marin's attack. With that as his only clue of where to lead the game, Jim made another move.

Again, Marin recorded the move, examined the position for a couple minutes and moved again. This time Jim almost jumped from his chair. The mistake was slight, only a tiny error and not just anybody could recognize it. Yet, Jim's memory bailed him out. He had played this ending against a Fide Master on the internet a few years back and although his mind refused to respond to calculation, the road to victory sat like a blueprint of recollection. He knew now that beating Marin might actually be possible, if he didn't mess it up.

Ten more minutes went by and Jim's head really started to sting now. He didn't know if he could finish the game. His moves rolled like an automaton, purely from memory, but he still had many to make before victory was final. The only good part now was that Marin's clock began to wind down. Back and forth they battled until there was only five minutes left on each side and that was when Jim saw something had changed inside his opponent. Marin seemed confused and his moves were starting to become strange.

Sure, he thought this kid might be a tactical genius, but his endgame certainly plagued him. This was typical of most junior chess players. They knew how to play the first half of a chess game, not the second half. The best strategy he knew now was to keep the endgame rolling, he had turned the tide on his aggressive opponent and now it was his turn to strike.

Methodically Jim's experience carried his position forward with every move and he watched 'Ticker' whittle away at Marin's valuable time. Still, Jim tried to make careful moves and checked everything carefully. When he grabbed a piece, he firmly placed it in the center of the board's square avoiding a disastrous slip at all costs.

Marin appeared to be flustered and in a hurry to move and that is when Jim knew that Marin would not recover. The boy just couldn't handle making good moves with so little time and the little red flag above 'Ticker' fell along with Jim's fatigued head. The game was officially over and he had defeated what he considered to be the strongest player he had ever faced.

Marin pulled his headphones off and stared at Jim in astonishment. "I should have won that game, man this thing is-" he tried to speak, but then stopped and shook his head in frustration.

"I don't think so," Jim lifted his head with serious effort. "No matter how well you play this endgame, I have a win here, I've played this line before and have it down. I don't have much energy, but I'll find a way to finish it out if you like?"

"Nah, I don't analyze games with anybody," Marin replied and got up quietly and left.

Jim looked around the room and it started to spin. He noticed the tournament director approach him, while a few players that watched the game gave him a pat on the back. It took a long time for him to focus his eyes and when finally he saw the room in a clear sense, it appeared empty. His game had been the last one completed.

"Great job Jim, perfect score," the tournament director announced and tried to shake his hand. "I'm just sorry that once again, you lose on tie-breaks. Dillard

Senior beat his son for a perfect score also, and you guys tie for first and he wins the tie. I'm really sorry."

Jim smiled and took a deep breath. He figured as much, but this time it didn't bother him, he beat Josh Marin a kid who certainly would be a world-class chess player in the future if trained properly. He seriously doubted either Dillard would have held a candle to Marin today. He got up and walked to the hotel front desk and paid to stay in the room another night. Dillards approached carrying a large trophy. They started to snicker at Jim.

"Poor Jim, thanks for taking down Marin for us. I guess you can't ever win on ties though?" Dillard Senior rubbed his words in.

"Why don't you just give up the game? You're never going to beat us," Terry followed.

Jim looked at them with a stern grin. "Next time we compete, things will be different," his head spun and he had to pause. "You know, I'm so sick of you two. Next time we meet things will be different."

Dillards laughed out loud, they couldn't believe what he had said.

"Jim," the tournament director called and hustled over to him. "Your first place share comes to over $500 dollars. Do you want me to write you out a check?"

"No," Jim choked out the word. "Make it out to the Flint Chess Team, on behalf of Junior Walters." He glared at the Dillards. "I don't want there to be any excuses for the Flint chess team to not show up to next year's state high school team championship. By the way coach," Jim looked Dillard Senior in the eye. "That trophy is the ugliest one I've ever seen, you can have it on tie-breaks. I have a better one at home anyway—My head hurts," he rubbed his temples quick and then walked away.

Both Dillard's eyes opened wide and the tournament director's jaw dropped down. They stood there stunned at Jim's donation and his words. They did nothing but watch him hobble to his room and shut the door behind him.

CHAPTER 16

▼

A NEW FACE

Jim opened his eyes and the world appeared fuzzy. He didn't know where he was and when his vision cleared he saw Greg sitting in a chair across from him. Greg noticed him awaken and left the room only to come back with Ole Cookie who had a cup of coffee in his hand.

"Jim, you're back!" Ole Cookie said and then called a nurse who scuttled in and did some routine checks on him.

"Where am I?" Jim asked but his throat barely let the words escape.

"Just relax Jim, you're at St. Francis Hospital. We hadn't heard from you in awhile and when we checked your house we knew something was wrong. I sort of broke your door down to get in." Ole Cookie looked at Greg and then at Jim. "I'll fix it later this afternoon if you don't mind."

Jim shook his head and his memory started to come back. He remembered sleeping for nearly three days at the tournament hotel. When they got upset with him, he somehow managed to drive home, but when he got back he had collapsed in his bed. From that point on, he remembered nothing.

A doctor entered the room and started to mumble fancy medical words and then looked up at the others. "He's through the worst of it folks. I do believe he's going to recover."

"What did I have?" Jim's mouth barely asked.

"Please, save your voice," the doctor insisted. "You basically had a bad cold. Unfortunately I believe you coupled it with poor nutrition, chills and possibly fatigue and it became much like pneumonia."

"Will he be okay?" Ole Cookie asked while he adjusted his 'Army' baseball cap tighter onto his head.

"Yes, as a matter of fact we'll do a few more tests and get some good soup and other light foods into him, maybe he can even go home soon," the doctor said and scribbled some data on a sheet of paper and then detached it and put it on a stand by the foot of Jim's bed.

Ole Cookie talked with the nurse and doctor some more about making sure Jim stayed healthy. Greg took the moment and walked over to his coach. His eyes were somewhat teary and he kept his distance. He was genuinely fearful for his chess mentor's health and his face betrayed every feeling.

Uncomfortable as well and not sure what to say, Jim blurted out the first thing he could think of, a chess move, "e4."

Greg stumbled back a step and his confusion disappeared. A smile reached his face. "Knight to f6," he replied.

"Alekhine's Defense?" Jim whispered. "When did you take that up?"

"I don't know," he reached his hand over and they gripped a handshake. "I guess I started playing that today," he said and took a deep breath of relief. He now felt everything might come back to normal.

*   *   *   *

The chess season started later than the players wanted. Ole Cookie got things up and running until Jim had recuperated enough to come back. It took Jim seven weeks to snap out of the tough spell he had endured and even at this point his weight remained 20 pounds below normal. Ole Cookie checked on him frequently at home and kept telling him about how great the chess team was going to be this year. Often Jim told him to quit teasing, because as much as he liked Craig Bellington, he knew the young man didn't have the chess strength to go all the way at States. Which was all right and understandable, but he didn't want any false expectations either. Ole Cookie didn't want to hear his pleas, and clucked off an order for him to remain silent, like Jim was a private. He insisted that a huge surprise awaited his arrival to the first club and absolutely refused to give him any idea as to what it was.

When the time came for that first meeting back, he used a cane for a little extra support. He couldn't believe at how weak physically he had become, but he also listened to his doctors and he listened to Ole Cookie. Moreover, he started to put the pain of losing Walters behind him and his spirit slowly began to return. Before he entered the biology room that held the chess club he could smell pizza. When he crossed the door he noticed they had several of them laid out with pop and other snacks. His players cheered him on and he entered waving hello. The feeling of seeing his players again drove good feelings through him and gave him the energy to come in and eat some goodies.

He sat down and looked at his players, and noticed they were all there, except Jeff of course. However, there seemed to be an extra person with an unfamiliar face in the room. Upon a clearer look, he noticed a foreign looking young man off to the side. The players picked up on this immediately and gave Jim their attention.

"Mr. B," Craig took the lead and said. "I have good news and bad news. How about the bad first?"

Jim nodded.

"The bad news is I don't think I'm going to be your fourth board this year."

Jim nodded again, not sure what he was saying.

"The good news is I make a great manager. We have a new person in the chess club this year."

"Yeah, his name is Wim Vanderfliert," Greg continued. "He's a foreign exchange student from the Netherlands and the school rules state that he's eligible to play for Escanaba!"

"And," Big Alan chose his turn to speak. "He can beat any of us in a three game match."

Wim displayed a strong case of shyness and Jim knew he'd get along well with this young man.

"We have four strong players Mr. B," Tyler took his turn to communicate. "We can beat Flint this year. Wim will take down Dillard while we take down the rest of Flint."

Jim sat dazed at the stroke of good fortune, but something inside of him kept him relaxed. His nerves were not a problem and as exciting as their prospects appeared, he didn't have the courage right now to tell them that Flint was the least of their worries with an incredibly strong Poly-Sci team out there waiting as well. Plus, he wanted to get away from winning as the sole concept anyway. He wanted excellence and he wanted to produce 'tough' chess players, not necessarily 'winning' ones. If they won games, great, but no way would he ever get burned worrying about winning chess tournaments or state titles again. The kids were what mattered most. The concept that these young players would grow up to be strong, good moral men, was what being a chess coach was about and that goal he intended to fulfill.

Jim came out of his daze and offered Wim a game. They set up the pieces and everyone watched to see how he would fare. The game progressed ten moves and Jim picked up fast on a positional idea. The boy played exceptionally strong and he could see the European style of chess in Wim. Ten more moves went by and the fortress around Wim's king began to crumble. Even the players around him could see that their new teammate didn't have the power to hold up against the old master. Jim's attack circled his opponent's forces one last time and then strangled them. Defeated, Wim looked Jim in the eye and gave a respectful nod. He had been totally outclassed, but played tough. He tipped his king over and resigned.

Everyone in the room took a deep gasp of breath. Wim didn't understand. Jim smiled and said, "One rule we have on this team, is that we don't resign, ever." Wim nodded his understanding and Jim continued, "I believe you'll do just fine. We need to order you up a shirt, you're on the team."

*   *   *   *

Jim's health stabilized to some degree, but he still felt weak physically. The chess practices with the kids did more healing than anything and as the months before States ticked away the players responded beautifully. Every single practice they grew stronger and stronger and this time he felt the momentum that Walter's had told him the first year team lacked. This team was much different, yet light years behind the likes of a Josh Marin. They worked hard, they had well mixed chemistry and best of all they got along better than any five young adults he had ever seen.

Wim especially started to pour on the extra practice and his chess strength soared. He was defeating Greg nearly three out of four games consistently, but instead of anger in competition, they worked to improve together and even Greg's game improved to the next level. They won all their games in the league and although undefeated, Greg had all but given up hope to retain first board when Jim surprised the team one evening at chess club and drew the players together for their final meeting before States.

"Guys," he said to them all in a serious tone. "We need to understand a decision I've made that I don't want to come back and haunt me later." He put his two fingers in the air and waved them back and forth a couple times from mild anxiety. "I want to say this right—We all know that Wim has the most strength on the team and first board is certainly within his rights and capability. However, when we go to States next week, our lineup is going to be Greg on first board, Wim on second, Big Alan and Tyler will be on third and fourth respectively. Craig, you have the management duties."

The players sat in confusion, not sure of what to make of the starting order until finally Greg asked, "Mr. B, why am I still on first if Wim can beat me? Shouldn't he get the top spot?"

The other players nodded in agreement.

"Normally yes," he paused and took a deep breath. The players noticed he was concerned about something. "Guys, we've run our course this year and our plan for States is set. I haven't exactly been one hundred percent open with you on every aspect." He paused. "I have always been honest, but I did leave out one important detail. I didn't tell you about a foe we're going to have to face down at States."

The boys just looked at him in bewilderment.

"There is a powerhouse team out there from the Poly Science Institute of Technology something or other, Poly-Sci they're known as and they are good. They beat Flint last year by a perfect sweep. They listen to classical music with headphones on while they play chess. Nearly every one of them is a genius and they're unstoppable. I played their first board last summer and he's a monster." He paused again and looked the boys in the eyes. "I feel a switching of player strategy might be our best bet against them. If we can dent them at second with Wim, maybe our one, three and four will get lucky and we can at least draw. It's our best chance, really our only chance in a very bad situation, at least mathematically speaking."

"Mr. B is that why you haven't given us a lot of details about States like you normally do?" Tyler asked.

"Yes. I've been excited to go, but you're right I just didn't want any of you to get any false hopes. I also want to be frank with you all as well. I don't want to go there just to win. Winning States is not what matters."

The boys almost laughed, but then they realized he was serious.

"Why go if we aren't trying to win Mr. B?" Wim asked. His accent dragged the words.

"Wim that's a great question. When the team started almost three years ago, my whole philosophy was to coach the toughest team. Somewhere I got away from that, that particular team got away from that. We started to play only to win and our wins not only turned into losses. We turned into weak players. Today this team is tough and all I want to ask of you is to play your best. If you guys promise to be the toughest team, I promise that it won't matter whether we win or lose. This is the only chance we have. It feels backwards, but our only path to victory is if we just go to play as hard as we can and not worry about the actual outcome."

The players sat quiet pondering Jim's words.

"Mr. B," Wim stood up and took a step forward, "I like that lesson and this is a good team. I would be honored to play second board for Escanaba."

"And I first," Greg added.

"Me on three," Big Alan followed.

"Four," Tyler chimed.

"Hey, I'm the manager, whatever you need, I'm there," Craig answered.

"All right guys, hands in a circle," Jim stated and the players listened. "Esky-chess Express is back on track. Next week whether it's the 'Tune-Heads' from Poly-Sci or Flint or both, the Escanaba Eskimos are going to be the toughest team at States."

"Yes! Eskychess Express!" The players exclaimed.

CHAPTER 17

▼

STATES—UNITED

The morning of the big state competition had arrived. The snow dropped a light coat like it seemed to do last time Jim was at this hotel. He felt good again to be in Detroit. The previous night he and the team showed Wim the smoothie tradition and how to eat good while later in the evening they swam in the pool. At breakfast he pounded the food, which if his doctor could have seen would have made him smile with glee. The mood of the team was nervous, but Jim's nerves didn't bother him.

When the team entered the cafeteria they brought their storage tote of equipment to a long table and pondered all the other teams around them. They didn't have any questions for Jim this time. The team was experienced and even with one new member, the background seemed to be something familiar, not alien. They even recognized the Dillards over in their normal corner, pondering over their precious laptop to try and get one more shred of analysis in before the matches officially began.

At another table Jim noticed the Birch Run team and their patented trench-coat look and then a slight shiver ran down his back. Not like full-blown nerves he used to have, but rather he thought he recognized one of the kids. After telling the players, they too realized that it was their old teammate Jeff!

"What the heck is he doing here?" Jim asked the rest of the team. "I thought he moved far away?" The team had no answers.

Craig came over and showed the Eskimos their first round pairing. Coincidentally enough they were the third ranked team, playing Birch Run at the start.

Why do these things have to happen to me? Jim thought, while a mild case of nerves took him. He fought them off and prepared his team for battle. Jeff or not, they had to be tough.

"These guys are no better than anyone else," Jim told them. "Toughest team, remember to be the toughest team. That is all you have to do."

The room filled up and the players found their spots. The Poly-Sci team took the first table, while Flint occupied the second. The Escanaba players took their third spot and Jeff grinned as he led his team into the room.

"Toughest team," Jim whispered one more time. The performance now was out of his hands. Everything was up to the players. The Birch Run coach tried to talk to him, but Jim politely shook hands with him and walked out of the playing room.

After an hour Tyler and Wim had thoroughly dominated their opponents and put the Eskimos up 2-0. Big Alan finished his opponent off in an endgame puzzle and Escanaba clinched the match point. But, Jeff and Greg clashed full force in their game and Jim started to worry that Greg might get worn down having such a tough opponent in the first round. To make matters worse, Jeff remained composed despite the rest of his team's losses and focused hard on one thing and that was to win his game.

Poly-Sci destroyed their first opponent while Flint followed suit a few minutes later. Escanaba had done much the same, except for the marathon game on first board. The game wound down to a couple minutes on each side, when Jeff started to look up at his coach. He then made a move and declared checkmate. In sporting fashion, he offered Greg a handshake that was accepted.

The cafeteria had a small stand that sold snacks and food and Jim led Greg over to the rest of the team who had decided to eat a light snack and rest at a nearby lunch table before the next round. Jim told them how proud he was of them and he directed his attention to Greg.

"Do not be ashamed of that game. Remember, he's an extremely good player. You played tough Greg. We won 3–1. On to the next opponent okay? I can't say this enough, just be tough! You were tough, you are doing it right, nothing to be ashamed of."

Greg still felt bad, but nodded an approval anyway. Birch Run's coach walked up behind Jim. He indicated that he wanted to talk. Jim followed him to the side of the room and saw Jeff standing there waiting.

"This young man," Birch Run's coach said, "would really like to have a word with you, would that be okay?"

Jim nodded his approval, but felt some nerves as well. Birch Run's coach gave Jeff a wink and a little pat on the back and then walked away to give them some privacy. The Esky players watched on though, to make sure Jeff didn't pull any funny business on their coach.

"Mr. B," Jeff said, but couldn't seem to get any more words out. The emotions on his face started to betray him.

"Nice game Jeff," Jim broke in, trying to ease the situation. "Greg is much stronger than last year, you must have been working on your game some."

"Everyday, that's all I do is practice chess. Who would have figured that?" he replied solemnly. "I was supposed to move out west, but my guardian sent me back to Michigan and Birch Run is where my Aunty is from. She took me in."

"How is everything going? New school and all?"

"Good, my Aunty takes better care of me than my guardian did. It's not always pretty, but it's actually fairly functional. I even made the B or better honor roll last semester."

"I'm glad to hear that Jeff. I really am."

"My coach is a pretty cool guy also. He's not as good as you at chess." Jeff and Jim both laughed.

"Or you either, I take it?" Jim quizzed back in fun.

"No, but he helps make sure I don't get into trouble."

Jim's nerves shrunk to nothing and he began to relax. The Eskimos watching could sense the same thing and started to come over to see their old friend.

"Mr. B—Guys," Jeff said and then paused, not sure of what words to choose. "I'm sorry for what I did to you guys." Jeff held his head down.

Big Alan gave him a pat on the back, while the rest of them smiled their support, "It's all right bud, we forgive ya."

"Jeff, I'm so glad things are working out for you." Jim offered him his hand and Jeff gave it a firm shake. "Good luck the rest of the tournament, and remember to be play tough."

"I will, and you guys try to give those top two monster teams something to remember from good old Escanaba okay?"

The rest of the team shook Jeff's hand and they instantly became motivated. The whole team, including Wim, felt like a big weight had been lifted from their shoulders. The depression of Greg's loss totally disappeared from their minds and round two was set to begin.

"Let's go get'em—Eskychess Express," Jim said and his team went into the tournament room fired up with unknown energy.

They crushed their second round opponents 4—0 and did the same thing the next round. They did it almost as fast as the best teams there and certainly made an impression on the Dillards. Everything went perfect that day and outside of Greg's loss to Jeff, they had a unique momentum. Exhaustion tired them beyond belief, but they held their heads high and stayed enthusiastic. They knew to ride this boost for whatever it was worth, because their scheduled fourth round opponent in the morning would be the strongest group of high school chess players Michigan had ever seen, the Poly-Sci 'Tune-Heads'.

CHAPTER 18

▼

THE TOUGHEST TEAM

Jim had a vivid dream that felt so real when he woke up he wasn't sure of his surroundings. He looked at the clock and realized the kids didn't need to be up for almost an hour yet and he could actually hear a couple of them snoring through the door of the suite. He decided to make a cup of tea by running water through the coffee maker without any filter or grounds. When the hot water started to run he just stared at it, while he visualized the dream again and tried to understand its meaning if indeed it had any.

He had been sound asleep for most of the night, but what he remembered most about the dream was that it took place at a tournament long ago that he and Walters had driven to. They had rode in the same old red Cutlass car they had used to travel to tournaments, but in the dream he was alone. Walters had won this particular tournament in reality and afterwards they went to a steak house and spent the winnings. The imagination of his dream forced him to trace all of Walter's games, move by move. The positions were crisp, as if he had walked into the very same tournament and played them himself. He was forced to be in Walters place and the winning moves flowed out of him naturally. Every game he tore through each opponent like Walters had done so many years before. At the end they gave him a big trophy and a check, which he accepted graciously, again like Walters did.

He pondered the dream over and over again, but could not make any understanding out of it. Finally the coffeemaker started to spurt as it ran all the water into the pot. He poured himself a cup and dipped his tea bag in.

"Walters," he called out quietly into the empty room. "Are we going to have a chance to win States today? Give me a sign, something, anything." Jim relaxed, but nothing happened. "Well, if there was a way back, Harry Houdini would have found it right?"

Just then the phone rang. He had lost track of the time. He picked it up and answered with surprise.

"Good morning," a soft voice replied, "this is your wake up call. Have a nice day sir."

He hung up the phone and looked at the ceiling. "Walters, was that you?" he called and smiled. "Darn you, I couldn't figure you out then and I still can't do it now. I don't know how we're going to get past the Poly-Sci team. It's going to be impossible. I suppose a miracle is never out of the question either. Walters, wherever you are, I give you my honest word, win or lose, this Eskimo team will be the toughest team that ever played high school chess."

✳   ✳   ✳   ✳

Jim cleaned up and got his players ready. He took them for pancakes and they ate like fiends. Fear started to show in their eyes. Jim understood they were mentally looking up at the equivalent of Mount Everest in terms of chess and he distracted them from those menacing thoughts.

"I remember once when I beat a 2400," he told them. "Greg you should have seen it, 99 out of 100 times that guy would have annihilated me. I was only rated 1700 then. But that one day, just that one day, I took him down."

The players listened and their ears perked up.

"Gentlemen, don't ask me why, but I know we're going to be tougher than the Poly-Sci team today. We have to be clever. Some way, somehow, we have to outwit them. I mean even if we lose, let's at the very least show them that Escanaba scrapped with a grizzly bear and even poked it around a little bit."

The players calmed their fear and the drowning mood changed to one of motivation. They paid their bill and headed to the tournament room. Inside they saw the coach-less Poly-Sci team sitting at a table, wearing their heavy sweatshirts with headphones wrapped around their necks. They looked so comical and so out of place. Nobody in their right mind would think of them as a group of chess geniuses. The cold facts though, were that they had never lost a game and their chess was some of the most potent around. The Esky players could hear them bragging about how after they won States this afternoon, they'd go to the national tournament and cause more terror there.

This sickened the Eskimos, but Jim just gave them a firm look and whispered to them. "Let's dent these boys. Let's be the tougher team, shall we?"

All the teams gathered to their tables. Escanaba took their perfect score against Poly-Sci while Flint took theirs against a strong Clio team that had all wins except for one drawn match the day before. The Eskimos glared at the 'Tune-Heads' but remained quiet. The Poly-Sci players quickly became uncomfortable and noticed the Eskimos unexpected determination.

Dillard Senior came over to Jim and showed him a line of statistics from a database on his laptop. "After you guys get killed, would you mind at least letting us look at your games, so we can try to put some sort of resistant up against them?"

"Mr. Dillard, you don't need to worry about Poly-Sci. You need to worry about the Escanaba Eskimos," Jim said in a cold manner and walked away.

Dillard Senior just shrugged off the comment. He would love to play a vulnerable Escanaba team in the last round instead of that blasted unbeatable Poly-Sci team. The tournament director gave the signal to begin and chess clocks across the room began to count down time.

The Eskimos opened solid, better than in any match they had played. Jim literally thought he saw eight grandmasters playing for the world championship. His players made no noticeable mistakes, but neither did the Poly-Sci players. The sight brought Jim back to his game last summer with Marin and how it was the same, they just didn't make a mistake and he doubted Greg could put up the same resistance he had, his players just didn't have the strength. At the same time he admired his boys, all he ever asked was for their best effort and this was definitely it. No matter what happened from this point on, he had achieved with his team what any coach ever desired, for his players to do their absolute best in competition.

An hour went by and the Eskimos pressed on, only to be matched step for step by the awesome strength of the Poly-Sci players. When hour number two went by the Escanaba players started to show signs of fatigue. The emotionless Poly-Sci team had gained a slight edge and the will of the Eskimos started to crack.

"They're grinding us down, Craig," Jim mentioned to the team manager shaking his head in remorse. "Wim is hurting the worst down a rook for a pawn. I figured with his masterful psychology he'd have had the best chance to win. Greg is down two pawns. Big Alan is down a knight and Tyler down two pawns. Wow, I've never seen anything like this. Darn it was a good run though."

Craig just sighed. He didn't totally understand the positions, but he kept seeing the pieces come off Wim's board and knew it was bad. Then something peculiar caught his attention and after a couple minutes went by, he noticed it again.

"Mr. B can I ask you a question?" he tapped on his coach's shoulder.

"Sure Craig, fire away."

"Well, I notice that every time Wim makes a move, his opponent puts his hand in his sweatshirt pocket. As a matter of fact, now I see Greg's opponent doing the same thing. They're all doing it now. Does that mean something?"

Jim's eyes opened wide as if he'd been struck by lightning. He was sure his heart had stopped. The whole situation thundered information in his brain and something he never even considered rang crystal clear in his mind.

"Oh my gosh Craig you just made the best move of the tournament," he whispered and then looked up at Dillard Senior who was a few tables over. "Dillard, give me that laptop now," he hollered.

"Sssh," some players from the room whispered.

"Sorry," he whispered back before the tournament director could chastise him.

Anger showed on Jim's face and Dillard Senior followed Jim's every command unsure of what was going on. The two moved to a quiet corner of the room and Dillard Senior popped open the fancy computer and loaded it up.

"Boot-up the strongest chess program you got on that thing, and do it now, there is no time to waste," Jim ordered.

Dillard Senior complied and within seconds a board with a welcome menu appeared. With a couple clicks of the touch-pad the machine was ready to play chess.

"Put it on think mode so I can see what it is thinking," Jim commanded further.

Dillard Senior obeyed and popped up a little window that showed the machine calculating moves and variations.

"Okay, I'm going to dictate the moves from my game versus Josh Marin last summer, you follow me and let's see what it thinks."

"Jim," Dillard Senior stopped him, "I have that game already in the database, we can analyze the whole thing in less than five minutes with this new program I have."

"Do it," Jim followed and the minutes started to count down on the analysis. He watched in despair as the life of his team was slowly being squeezed from it.

"Can't you get that thing to hurry up?" Jim asked impatiently.

"Why?"

"Don't you know?" he asked and took a breath. "Poly-Sci is cheating! They're not listening to music under those headphones. Those things aren't radios, somehow they're getting cues from a computer chess program."

Dillard Senior's eyes opened wide like Jim's had earlier and words wouldn't leave his mouth. Just then the computer spit out the analysis of the game. Sure enough to Jim's accusation, the computer predicted every single one of Josh's moves, up until the end where there was not enough time for him to seek the computer's aid.

"I can't believe it, do you know what this means? My Flint team will get last year's championship on a protest!"

"I'm not worried about last year's championship, I'm worried about this year's championship!"

Jim went over to his team and they could see something troubled him. "Escanaba players, I've never supported breaking a rule in match play ever, but whatever the consequence is I need you to take it. As your coach I am telling you not to make another move until I say so."

Bewildered, the Escanaba players didn't know what to make of the scene. However, they trusted their coach and folded their arms and sat motionless watching their clocks tick away. Wim smiled, as the task was easy for him, only his king remained. The tournament director stormed up to Jim and demanded an explanation of his outburst.

"They're cheating!" Jim hollered with anger and excitement all in the same tone. "They're not listening to music, they're somehow taking prompts from a chess computer hooked up through their headphones."

"How do you know that? Do you have any proof?" The tournament director countered.

"Check their pockets, let's see their music CDs."

The tournament director asked to see what was in their pockets, but Marin refused and the other players followed his lead.

"I can't force them to do it, it's against their rights. We're not policemen here. I'm sorry."

"Oh come on," Jim snapped. "Think about it, all the perfect scores they've had. Do you really think there are four high school players in the nation that are that good all from the same school district? Isn't that just a little bit too much of a coincidence? Where's their coach? They don't even have one do they? I smell a big rat here."

The Poly-Sci player's faces turned white. They knew they were caught, but rode the protection of the tournament director's support of not forcing them to be searched.

"Jim, okay you might be right," the tournament director pondered, but then shrugged his shoulders. "Still I can't make them empty their pockets. I had a law class once and I don't want to get sued or anything like that."

The Esky players just sighed in disbelief. They now knew everything that was going on and wanted to continue without the other team using a computer. Their clocks started to tick down to a couple minutes left and their concern for finishing on time grew.

Jim thought hard for a moment, not sure of what to do. The match was over. Esky was beat. He could think of nothing but packing his team up and taking them home. The situation was a shame. Suddenly an idea struck him from nowhere.

"All right then listen," he argued. "It's in the rule book that you the tournament director can order a player not to use a musical device if it bother's their opponents. I am lodging a formal complaint. Their music is too loud and it's distracting my players. I demand they put away their headphones."

Josh Marin's eyebrows lifted high with surprise, he knew he was checkmated with a verbal argument. The rules were clear on headphones. During play, if requested to take them off, it was irrelevant whether they were too loud or not, the rule had to be followed.

"Now that I can do," the tournament director replied with a grin and turned to the Poly-Sci team. "This coach has a complaint that your music is too loud, please remove your headphones for the remainder of the game."

The Esky players smiled at their coach's success and Jim nodded for them to begin playing again. The tables immediately turned and Poly-Sci's second board stalemated Wim on the very next move, Big Alan and Tyler rallied quick and made tremendous comebacks and won both games while Greg immediately gained a massive attack on Josh Marin.

The Poly-Sci team turned out to be nothing more than a sham. In actuality they barely knew how to move the pieces. For added punishment, Greg pushed pawns to the back rank and instead of making queens with them he took four bishops and inflicted an embarrassing and disgraceful 'Killer Bees' checkmate on his opponent.

Escanaba had done it. They had taken down the toughest chess team in existence, not with chess smarts, but by street smarts. Even the Flint team stood back stunned as Poly-Sci fell for the first time. The Esky players jumped up and down for joy and kept messing Craig's hair up.

"Swirley for the manager!" Big Alan joked with extreme delight.

Craig's eyes went wide until he realized they weren't really going to drown him in the boy's bathroom.

The rest of the players laughed in good humor.

Jim gave them all a pat on the back and congratulated them, but he turned his attention over to the Flint team. The Eskimos followed his eyes and stopped celebrating. They knew this tournament wasn't over yet.

CHAPTER 19

▼

THE CHAMPIONSHIP BATTLE

The intensity in the air could be felt. Not much time had elapsed and Dillard Senior was already rallying his troops. The astonishment of Escanaba's improbable victory had any easy explanation and the abrupt attention Flint normally would have given Poly-Sci, now focused solely on the Eskimos. The tournament director put up the pairings and they had the two remaining undefeated teams on Table 1. The Poly-Sci team couldn't be found and word went around the tournament that they went home in shame.

Jim huddled his players together. Although he felt quite fine himself, he saw the nerves rattle inside his players.

"Look guys," he told them. "I know I'm not the one to really give speeches. I rarely ever win round five games myself. I've lost more state titles in the last round than anybody I've ever met."

"What if we lose?" Tyler looked up at him. "I mean, we'll play tough, but we only won the fourth round because of luck."

"Yeah, this team is ready for us," Greg added. "Do you think they'll play the 'Grob' on us again?"

"No Greg, I don't think so. I have an idea that their strategy is to go head to head with us, straight up."

"Why?" Tyler asked. "Outside of Wim, they know they can psyche us out. Our team has a history of choking when it comes to winning the big game."

Jim mumbled a fake laugh. His players were defeated before they had even started the last round and he had to change that fact.

"Well, let's ask Wim how he feels. He reads the psychology of players better than any young player I've ever seen," Jim told them. "Wim, what do you think their strategy is for us?"

Wim shook his head; he didn't know what to say.

"Exactly Wim," Jim nodded. "Wim's right, they don't have a distraction this time."

Wim's eyes widened, but then he understood his coach's strategy and nodded back like he knew the right answer all along.

"They don't have a trick or a trap," Jim continued. "They are banking on us overreacting to them. What have they done to us before?"

"Some trick, a weird opening," Greg answered.

"That's right, and if I know Coach Dillard and his playing style after all these years, he's going into this thing head first. That is his trick this time, to not play any tricks. He's not going to do anything out of the ordinary this time, because he's hoping we error by chasing something that really isn't there."

The player's eyes lit up. The theory made sense.

"What do we do to stop them?" Greg asked.

"We change nothing," Jim said and stared at them for a second. "Don't worry about any tricks this time, they don't have them. We do nothing different from our preparation and we'll have a chance to win this thing. No matter what happens though, remember I'm proud of each and every one of you. Winning or losing the title doesn't matter. You have to believe me. Being the tougher team though, now that means everything. Eskychess-Express, let's give it to them."

The Eskimos once again lost their fear and felt good about entering the game. The tournament director had called all the teams into the playing room to begin the final round. The Flint players were already at Table 1 when the Eskimos joined them. The room settled and then the tournament director gave a few last minute announcements and invited everyone to the awards ceremony following the last game. He next gave the go ahead for everyone to begin and they did.

The games started and Jim felt calm inside, almost too calm. He thought for a moment on the feeling and there were no worries in him. The season would be over soon and no matter what it was successful. He looked over at Craig who shook with excitement and then left the room and went down to the cafeteria to get a cup of stale coffee. Normally he didn't care for the stuff, but today he enjoyed its bitter taste. He glanced at the cross-table along the way and calculated in an instant that if the match turned out to be a draw that Flint would win the title on tie-breaks. This was nothing knew to him, he knew that if the Eskimos were going to bring home a state championship, it would have to be by winning it outright. He decided not to watch the games, but rather relax on a table outside the playing room. His job was over. Everything was up to the players now. He could do no more.

Birch Run's coach sat down and talked to him for a minute and soon after Jeff came out of the playing room giving a thumbs-up sign. He had won his fifth game in a row and attained a perfect score on first board.

"Congratulations," Jim told Jeff and the two embraced in a firm handshake, while Birch Run's coach gave Jeff a pat on the back.

"Sure glad we got him this year Jim," the coach replied with his scratchy voice, "he really made it a great year for us."

Jim looked Jeff in the eye, "I'm glad he finally came around. It's not so bad being a good guy is it Jeff?" he asked the proud young man.

"No it's not," Jeff replied and smiled with genuine happiness. "Good luck Mr. B, I really hope you guys win it all this year. I'll be rooting for you dudes all the way."

"Thanks Jeff. You really gave us a positive boost yesterday. Like your play, I'm just hoping they're going to be the toughest team when this is all done."

"They will be Mr. B, they will be," he said and then walked off with his coach.

Wim then came out of the room and put a finger in the air, signifying one point. Jim took a deep breath and relaxed. The win put the Eskimos in a 1—0 lead. Wim sat by Jim and Tyler came out shortly.

"A draw," he mentioned to Jim. "Big Alan has a dead draw too, we have them tied no matter what," he said and then paused. "Let me guess, we lose on tie-breaks?"

"You bet we do," Jim grinned. "How's Greg's game going?"

"He's down a pawn, but playing hard," Tyler answered. "You were right they did nothing to surprise us this time. It's straight up chess. I don't think Coach Dillard is too pleased."

"He's pleased Tyler," Jim looked back, but stayed calm. "The state championship is in his son's hands. That's all he asks for."

"True," Tyler said and nodded his understanding.

Big Alan then came out of the playing room with a scowl on his face. "A draw, dang it, I just couldn't punch that pawn in on him."

"Don't worry Big Al, everything is okay," Jim talked with calm words.

"I checked Greg's game before I left, he's down two pawns now. Still lots of pieces though. All he needs is a draw."

They all sat quietly, almost knowing the situation would end up in another tie and they'd get yet another uninspiring second place finish due to a couple of mathematical points. The game continued and continued and the Eskimos just sat and exercised patience. Suddenly, Jim saw some commotion going on in the tournament room and stood up. Greg was pacing behind his table, pulling at his hair upset and almost in tears. Jim told his players to remain seated and bolted into the room to see what happened. At first sight he saw Dillard Senior with a wide smile on his face.

"Your player just dropped a rook," he snickered in a whisper.

Greg paced back and forth like he had lost a wallet with a thousand dollars in it. He looked at Jim and then stammered some more. Terry Dillard soaked up every bit of Greg's misery.

Jim looked down at the position and a chessboard appeared instantly in his mind. He analyzed every possibility of the position and saw that the game was hopeless for Greg. Every move sequence seemed to win for Terry. The obvious unprotected rook capture seemed to be the quickest way to defeat, but Jim's intuition expressed caution. Something about that piece held a strange mystique and he analyzed the move deeper and deeper. He calculated an odd series of moves and then his breathing jumped with excitement. Finally, he followed all the continuations in his mind to the end and learned Greg's trick.

The free rook happened to be a well-baited psychological trap and that Greg's emotional performance was a mere act, a ruse. He could see everything clear now. Greg was trying to get Terry Dillard emotionally fooled into accepting the Greek Gift and six deceptive moves later he would force checkmate on his unsuspecting victim. It was an excellent last hope, Greg's position was busted and this was the chess version of a 'Hail Mary' pass.

Greg finally sat back down and cupped his ears with his hands. His face showed defeat. "Yeah, I refuse to resign," he told Terry with scorn. "Just like you guys I'm not allowed to do it."

Terry Dillard laughed at his helpless opponent. With a big smile on his face he swallowed his opponent's rook with his knight. Without thinking, Greg carefully slid his other rook to the e3 square and slammed his fist on the clock. He could barely breath and his body began to shake. His eyes stayed wide and in five more moves he'd have Escanaba's nemesis checkmated once and for all.

Jim smiled and looked at Flint's coach. He whispered, "Mr. Dillard, I promise I didn't teach him how to be a good actor. Your boy fell for a trick this time and will be checkmated in five moves. Congratulations on your second place finish."

Dillard Senior's smile turned to a frown. He grunted and realized he too had fallen for Greg's trick and could see the loss play out in his mind. Jim walked out of the room while Greg crushed Flint's final hopes for the state title.

"Well?" the rest of team asked with impatience when Jim walked out of the playing room.

"Gentlemen," he said and curled his lip. "We just won a state title!"

At that moment Greg burst through the door and grabbed his coach from behind and put him in a big hug. "I did it, he's checkmated, the game is over!" he yelled.

The rest of the players joined in and their excitement rose above all levels. After all the trials and tribulations the Escanaba Eskimos had endured, they became the Michigan State High School Chess Champions for the year 2007!

$$* \qquad * \qquad * \qquad *$$

The awards ceremony went smooth. The Esky players remained on cloud nine. The feeling of being a champion was surreal. Jim had waited his whole life for such a moment and it had finally arrived. Now that it was complete, he felt so happy that he was able to share this joy with this exact group of kids. The struggles had been worth the effort.

Wim received the top second board trophy, and shook hands on the podium with Jeff who had earned the top first board trophy. Following the individual performance awards was the presentation of team trophies, to which the tournament director gladly awarded the first place trophy to the Escanaba Eskimos. He announced that he thought last year's performance by Poly-Sci was the best he'd ever seen, but on this occasion it was truly his privilege to watch a team with such fire and determination overcome all odds to gain victory.

Dillard Senior even walked up to Jim this time and gave him a real handshake. "Well done Jim, I've never seen anything like you. I didn't get to thank you for the donation last summer, but thanks."

Jim couldn't keep the smile off his face, but he shook his opponent's hand and bid him farewell. The team said goodbye to Jeff and the Birch Run team and then packed up the van for their trek home. The 10-hour ride went by much faster than normal and the team kept stopping at fast food restaurants to get burgers and milk shakes to drag it out. The team even let Craig have a cola flavored ice cream drink instead of cherry. Nobody wanted this night to end.

Finally, at 4:00 AM in the morning, they arrived back in Escanaba. There were no fire-trucks with lights waiting for them; there were no police cars with sirens. There was no celebration of any sorts. The only praise they'd get would be a nice little article in the local newspaper about the successful title run. Instead, happy parents with a loud yelp from Ole Cookie greeted them when they arrived in the school parking lot and all the players quietly went home with their parents, happy as could be.

To the members of the Escanaba Chess Team, they had won the biggest contest they had ever faced in the chess arena. The 'Super-Bowl' of high school chess was complete and they had memories of it to last a lifetime. They had lived a dream that had the odds of one in a million. Odds that were overcome, because a young man named Jim Berzchak prompted by his best friend Junior Walters, decided to accept the invitation from a group of youngsters to teach and coach the game they all loved. In the end, the Eskimos lived a wonderful dream and they all grew to become not only great chess players, but also strong young men that valued their society and cherished their culture. The Eskychess-Express had reached its destination and delivered its goods.

EPILOGUE

▼

During end of the school year, the Eskimos had gained such a popular standing within the small community that fundraisers were held for the team to compete in the National Chess Team Competition. They went undefeated with two draws and placed 6th overall in the nation and won instant recognition of being the 'Little Toughest Team'. For once, tie-breaks had no bearing on their result. A local businessman and chess lover anonymously donated a generous sum of money to have a huge celebration banquet and a special plaque was created for all the players and their coach to remember their championship triumph. Jim put his plaque next to his 1989 trophy on the mantle.

Wim went back to Europe and attended a private college in Oslo. Big Alan and Tyler went to Michigan Tech University and were roommates in the dorms. Big Alan entered electrical engineering while Tyler went into Economics. Craig joined the Air Force and before he left he reunited his Uncle Brad and Jim, who celebrated the team's big victory one evening and played chess for nearly 10 hours. Jim did not lose a game.

Jeff surprised everyone with a letter, stating that he had received a full ride scholarship to Western Michigan University. The scholarship pertained to Western's Criminal Justice Department and if Jeff successfully completed the program, there was a special option to pay for his police academy. After his first semester he had a 4.0 grade point average and his attitude remained very positive.

Greg stayed home after graduating high school and attended Bay College, the same school his father worked at. The college had a tuition reimbursement program for children of full time employees and this gave Greg a great chance to get college credit and earn some money working in the cafeteria with his dad. His plans after Bay were to go to the University of Michigan and enroll in the aerospace engineering program.

With tears in his eyes, Jim quietly ended the chess program at Escanaba to everyone's shock. Since all his players graduated high school, this presented a good opportunity to stop the team without leaving any younger players hanging. He then announced that he was going to Northern Michigan University in Marquette to become a teacher in home economics, which surprised even himself when he chose it, but seemed most logical because of his cooking experience. He promised that when he received his teaching license and landed a job, he'd once again start a scholastic chess program.

While attending Northern he met a nursing student his age named Sandra also from Escanaba. Although she had never heard of the chess team, Jim had no problems filling her in on all the details. In time they grew closer and Jim drew up enough courage to ask her on a date, which she accepted with happiness.

The pain Jim felt of losing Walters healed a bit with the passage of time and Sandra's companionship. Many nights though he sat out on his dock and thanked his friend for everything he'd done for him. Many times he'd find himself looking at his championship plaque and still not believing that his team had placed first. He felt fulfilled. His premise held, chess like any other sport wasn't about winning or losing, it was about achieving excellence and being the toughest performer in competition. The Eskychess Express was the toughest ride he'd ever taken and it was worth it all. He knew he'd coach a new chess team real soon.

0-595-34630-8

Printed in the United States
55407LVS00005B/51